Interiors

Wolfgang Georg Fischer

Interiors

A Novel Set in Vienna 1910-1938

TRANSLATED FROM THE GERMAN BY INGE GOODWIN
IN COLLABORATION WITH THE AUTHOR

Peter Owen · London

ISBN 0 7206 0371 4

Translated from the German *Wohnungen*

PETER OWEN LIMITED
12 Kendrick Mews Kendrick Place London SW7

First British Commonwealth edition 1971

Printed in Great Britain by
Clarke Doble & Brendon Ltd Plymouth

1 Inner Town (First Premises)

The Schottenring, which has no connection at all with Scotland, much less with rings or jewellery, is easy to find if you come to Vienna, bear right from the University across the Ring towards the Danube Canal, and keep a careful eye on the street signs: there it is, black on white in an oval frame, SCHOTTENRING.

Grandfather-architects (juggling wildly with acanthus, scrambled-egg frieze, chequerboard patterns and Renaissance garlands as their sons might with school dusters) planted the Schottenring with mansions in the Ringstrasse style: granite and sandstone caryatids with granite and sandstone bosoms, balconies with amphorae, roofs topped by obelisks, lion's head doorknockers for lawyers' apartments, a marble Hercules fronting the porter's lodge with its spyhole—behind which the Bohemian caretaker sits, watching, spying, speculating about the figures that walk across the red carpet to the lift, push numbered brass buttons and then, amid sedate thunder, bourgeois witches without broomsticks, steel-cable-creaking, magically freed from gravity, disappear up the lift-shaft.

What are bourgeois witches doing in Ringstrasse-style mansions, rising up lift-shafts like municipal blood corpuscles to the fourth or the sixth floor, laboriously sliding shut the lift door with its brass handles and clanging home the lift gate? Alarm signal for the ears of the spy on the ground floor: getting out on the sixth floor—a model; on the fifth floor—a client; on the fourth—a patient; getting off on the third floor—an articled clerk; and on the first floor—a visitor for the Baron.

Leave out the second floor. That is the mystery level, my own floor of fears and inhibitions. I will not let the glances and thoughts of the Bohemian spy on the ground floor pass here, I shall hold the rattling lift gate shut, and the bourgeois witches without broomsticks riding up and down all day long will have to find another exit; they can go through the roof, for all I care, and ogle the asphalt-coloured bosoms of the façade-caryatids from on high; or let them crawl away and hide under greasy brown blankets in the porter's lodge like the Bohemian's black tomcat. Why the hell can't they stay in some coffee-house by the Stock Exchange across the Ring, put their last pence into shares of the second oldest steam railway line in Austria, the only major line still in private hands, the Südbahn? I shall not let anyone get out here, I shall keep the shaft gate closed and shut the lift door on everyone's fingers. I have good reasons for it. This second floor of the Ringstrasse house on the Schottenring is my starting-point, the first of my show-apartments, the Start.

After all, who wants to be disturbed in the starting position? Do you know any runners who surround themselves with old school pals, aunts and uncles, all their good, worthy, dear and beloved acquaintances, at the start of a race? Every trainer will tell you that the starting position must be taken seriously. I have padlocked the gate of the lift-shaft with an Imperial Customs seal, until I can be sure that you have thoroughly taken in this first apartment-setting. Which is not so simple, because there are really two settings, two doors to the landing, two apartments, within the one apartment. Or you could call it one floor with two apartments, it all depends, two make one, or one makes two: the sorcerer's multiplication table of the speculative boom of the eighties—nought makes infinity is no longer in fashion. Anyhow, there are two of everything. Two entrance halls; two lavatories; two minute servants' rooms; two men of importance, the Imperial and High Court Advocate who keeps the family, and the lover; two children; two servants, three if you include the nurserymaid (a slight flaw in my calculation); two entrances, or two exits, as required; two religions—the Judaism of the parents, the Roman Catholicism of the children, who don't, however, represent two sexes (they are both boys); two musical pieces of furniture, the piano with its velvet cover, and the lute to which the reddish-blonde lady of the house sings Schubert-lieder when her lady friends come on Friday evenings; two glass cabinets, with silently barking porcelain dogs, laughing little fake Chinamen squatting in Turkish or Buddha position, folds of fat slanting across their badly carved bellies; china shepherdesses with pink frilly parasols; a bust of white, snowy-white, bisque, a young and handsome Emperor Franz Joseph, and its companionpiece—I will not betray the subject, an unhappy Empress.

Also two swelling balconies with amphora-balustrades (one can only just stand on Ringstrasse balconies—they are too small for sitting down on—like a general, or an archduke, a Somebody in the Great Empire, taking the salute at a parade). The Imperial and High Court Advocate occasionally steps out on to one or other of these, in mufti, to snatch a bit of fresh air and to look down, from one balcony to the Danube Canal, from the other to the brick edifice of the Stock Exchange. Viewed from a certain angle, his position on a balcony is at the same time a public stance. Roman ornaments and Greek lines of Stock Exchange architecture, a bourgeois game of world empires, erected twenty years after the 1848 revolution. Here, you could say with pardonable pride, a position has been established. As for the other balcony, with its view of the Danube Canal—why, one could buy a ticket from the Danube Steamship Navigation Company, go on board and, smoking Virginia cigars, listening to the lapping of the waves, past Pressburg, past Budapest, past flying cormorants and dancing peasants in Romanian national costume, drift down as far as the Black Sea . . . one might do that, and establish yet another pattern, that of a Grand Tourist.

The apartment is divided into two parts. The domestic part with piano and lute and porcelain Chinamen, and the Advocate's office. Clients use the left-hand door on the landing, ring the brass bell, are admitted and led to the antlered clothes-stand to disrobe. The right-hand door is used by tradesmen, governesses, the lover, the two boys use it when they come back from Catholic instruction in the afternoon, and relatives on a visit from a small Moravian ghetto. There the synagogue façade is as handsome and yellow and baroquely round-windowed as the castle chapel at Schönbrunn, a feudal parallel as pleasing as the story of that ghetto's foundation : The Count of Lissitz swaps the Count of Lomnitz two Jew families for two pairs of hounds. These two Jew families with their canine pedigrees were, as the Count humorously puts it, the beginning of his Mosaic kennels. It is from these kennels that the relatives come to Vienna, use the right-hand landing door, are swiftly admitted and concealed: provincial air is none too sweet.

An aunt from the provinces (Aunt Esterl, for instance, sister of the Imperial and High Court Advocate) sits on the period sofa with its red cherrywood legs and green gold-bordered stripes on a white rep cover, gazes about the drawing-room, sees the upturned beribboned lute atop a felt cloth on the black-ice mirror of the Bechstein grand piano, the porcelain Chinamen in the glass cabinet, possibly even the shadow of asphalt-grey bosoms of the façade-caryatids dancing over the honey-waxed polish of parquet flooring, takes a deep breath and says to her relatives, who have nothing to say, 'Go on, tell me about all the grand people here. After all, you do live in a great city!'

Listen, Aunt Esterl (unfortunately no one in the family found the courage to say so), this residential set-up on the Vienna Schottenring, obliquely facing the brick Stock Exchange and near the Danube Canal, is in itself a part, a model, a Platonic allegory of Society. Instead of telling you school anecdotes about your converted, though still circumcised nephews, or talking about the love-affairs of your beautiful sister-in-law, or the most recent appearance of the Emperor and his consort in the Royal Box of the Imperial Opera House, I prefer to describe for you the ground plan of the twin-entranced apartment which belongs to your brother, Imperial and High Court Advocate in Vienna—*ad cognoscendum genus humanus sufficit una domus*—and the grandeur of high society is really no greater than this.

This drawing-room with its two tall windows flanked on the inside by draped dark-red curtains, their exterior guarded by granite and sandstone caryatids, this room lumbered with period furniture, soothed by an imitation Tabriz rug, frightened by the music-breathing Bechstein grand, at times disturbed by the clatter of a tea-trolley entering with coffee-pots concealed under pink-lined cosies, heaped with nut-strudel, bearing doughnuts, pregnant with hams and stuffed with chicken legs, and laughed at by porcelain

Chinamen this drawing-room, then, is matched by an equally large room on the opposite side of the stone-tiled landing.

The office of the Imperial and High Court Advocate: identical caryatid guards for the windows, the same curtains, only in brown, a desk oppressive as a bad conscience, with Gothic Revival serpentine carvings ornamenting the corners, a green baize cloth to cover the bald patch, and a photograph of the lady wife: Mama with the two boys in sailor suits (docile as lambs and equally spotless), all three enshrined in a velvet frame inscribed, By Appointment to the Imperial Court, Court Photographer Charles Scolik, Vienna VIII, *vis-à-vis* the Piarist College; ink-stand with silver cover—uncover your head and down on your knees, Imperial and High Court Advocate, not dragooned to prayer by military order, but in front of every client, while the pen with its black mouth-nib rests, discreetly not recording this symbolic prostration. Behind the desk, the tall chair whose carved upper edge all but touches the righteous sky above the capital city and metropolis; a secular, rabbinical throne, seat of judgment and of learning, the crucial piece of furniture, omphalos of the office, navel of the Empire's Civil Code, centrepiece of the body of statutes —projecting above the head of the seated Imperial and High Court Advocate, and itself only overshadowed by the jointed armour (roll-front patent) of the filing-cabinet behind it: a powerfully staged climax to this furniture drama.

If you, Aunt Esterl, would care to roll up that protective armour and join me in tossing the files joyfully up into the air—there you have the susurrus of this great society, all neatly tied up in bundles. The case of Gehmacher v. Simmlinger: sharp practices in wangling municipal contracts—

ugh, disgusting. Rosenkranz v. Porges: textile trade swindle in Vienna's Rag Trade district. Lichtblau v. Höllwöger: a quarrel between architects, jealousies among the incompetent, against a background of sly anti-semitism. And here this fat bundle, the Estate of the brewer Geistinger, deceased: a man from the dregs, who rose to the top on floods of foaming, hissing, brown hop and malt derivatives, bought land beyond the Outer Lines and sold at the right time to speculative builders—a time when mansion flats were much in vogue—and who also owned forests and uncultivated fields, and left no issue, only three mutually hostile sisters, who brought us into the matter, albeit somewhat belatedly.

Then next door the dining-room; the dining-table seating six can be drawn out like an apple-strudel to accommodate eight, twelve at a pinch. Never twenty-four, however. The number 24 somehow signifies a more than bourgeois household, and must therefore remain taboo. Has anyone ever heard of a carriage or sledge pulled by twenty-four white horses drawing up in front of this Ringstrasse house? Never has there been occasion to use a breakfast service of twenty-four settings. Such high-life fantasies merely flit through the mind of the Imperial and High Court Advocate's wife—perhaps that is why her lover, who occasionally uses the right-hand entrance along with governesses and tradesmen, is a noble '*von*', a commodore in the Imperial Navy.

Aunt Esterl is perfectly content with the dining-room as it is: the table which can seat twelve, the sideboard with glass-fronted cabinet above, elaborate ornamental key with yellow tassels dangling, long-stemmed wine glasses within and the special gold-rimmed dinner service, the sort of glasses to be seen in the picture behind the table, rubbing shoulders with a curved sabre reflecting the sunlight, a red fez and a bijou plaster reproduction of the Venus de Milo. Spirals of bright lemon peel, too—an Interior after the Oriental fashion (as the academician Professor Hippenpferdl explained when he brought this picture along in settlement of his outstanding bill—even artists have lawsuits); above the table, a cut-glass chandelier, a crystal marvel just like the one in the Royal Box at the Opera, or the Spanish Court Riding School, just as in all the great houses, but smaller.

The dining-room is matched by a room of equal size on the other side of the landing. This is again a lawyer's office, with furnishings as before: desk of oppressive conscience, jointed-armour filing-cabinet, inkwell with lid, bearded man on a tall chair (the brother of the Imperial and High Court Advocate next door). As I said before, there are two of everything. The two brothers share the offices, the rent, the typists' wages, the stamping pads, the black-and-yellow tape used for tying up files and sealing documents; stamp duty is paid by the client, or else concealed among the total costs if he is to be kept happy for the sake of future lawsuits. The room next to this is a Civil-Service-utilitarian replica of the two offices. This is where the articled clerk—fresh from his law degree—sits waiting for the smaller fry among the clients.

Transfer the ground plan of the clerk's office across the landing and it becomes a square of bedroom. High, old-fashioned walnut bedsteads piled with downy bedclothes, four bow-fronted cupboards for linen and clothes, a white-painted wash-stand with china water-jug, windows curtained with fluttering white muslin, a bell-pull on the centre of the wall above the beds. Pull the bell-rope and—such are the fantasies of the lady of the house in half-sleep—either the fragrant linen-cupboard opens and from behind the mirror, trailing clouds of lavender, enters the Imperial Naval Commodore, the nobleman, the lover, in his snow-white, starched, full-dress uniform, who bows briskly, parades around the square of the conjugal bed, comes to a halt in front of the sleeping husband, whips out his dress sword and fatally stabs the Imperial and High Court Advocate. Or—acting out the thoughts of the master of the house now half-dozing—the wardrobe opens and out comes Solomon, teacher of rabbinity, from the Moravian ghetto, Aunt Esterl's father, his own father, and throws and throws and throws Catholic chasubles, bishops' mitres, Capuchine and Benedictine habits, gold-embroidered baroque vestments and black nuns' robes, on to conjugal beds, and on to this mound of clothing he throws a seven-branched candelabrum. The whole lot flares up in flames. Actually, only a domestic—the cook, or the chambermaid—should appear when one pulls the bell-rope. The nobleman in his dress uniform and the raging Solomon in his wrath make an ill-assorted couple.

A better-matched couple may be seen in those photographs on the bedside tables, separated though they are by two gleaming white widths of beds: more precisely, on the marble top of the lady's bedside table, the master of the house, the husband, the Imperial and High Court Advocate, complete with grey fur-lined and fur-collared overcoat, walking-stick hooked over his left arm, pince-nez on his nose and a bowler on his head; on the bedside marble top beside the master's pillow, a carved watch-stand and a portrait of the lady, cradling her lute, a Makart-style* bouquet and a deep mysterious gaze to match. Why, as Aunt Esterl might well ask—and she does ask the most impossible questions—

* Hans Makart, the fashionable painter who gave his name to a certain lush style of interior decoration and female beauty.

why not the Imperial Naval Commodore in his full-dress uniform on this marble top, and over there, two bed-widths away, the raging Solomon with his blazing candelabrum? Let me tell you: it's on account of the boys in sailor suits. Honour thy father and thy mother, but not necessarily the naval commodore in white full-dress or grandfather Solomon with the seven-branched candelabrum. Think about the latter as little as possible anyhow: for Schottenring children the Moravian ghetto is too far afield for an excursion. We do not call there, least of all in our sailor suits. Solomon may be a perfectly good name for the Old Testament, but it doesn't exactly smooth your career in the multiracial Empire—albeit in this case it withers on a parched, unbaptised branch of the family tree. Surely you don't want to be seen in the Corpus Christi Procession—His Holy Apostolic Majesty Franz Joseph actually walking under the canopy—limping after the group of pious Schotten College scholars, with Solomon's seven-armed candelabrum? Why all this grandiloquence in the bedroom? Mere bedroom tales these, and as usual unsubstantiated.

I had better open the second bedroom door, a wallpaper-covered door slightly stained with brown, and advance into the minor labyrinths of the apartment. These comprise the nursery, the servants' rooms, kitchen and bathroom. The latter is squeezed in like a hosepipe between bedroom and nursery, and contains a boiler, the size of a locomotive, covered in peeling oil paint, black and white tiles, no window, only a small ventilator flap leading into the light-shaft. The family's bath towels and hand towels hang like temple robes on brass hooks; toothbrushes, sponges with enlarged pores, jars of bath-salts—everything has its place, there is nothing unusual, no recesses or mirror surfaces for acting out daydreams; neither the melodramatic nonsense of the bedroom, nor the furniture-confrontations of the office. Nevertheless, it is precisely the bathroom which Aunt Esterl most admires. It strikes her as the heraldic beast of the upper bourgeoisie, lying there with its bathtub-tail, its infinitely extended trunk-pipes sipping crystal-clear mountain spring water from the snow-covered Rax and the icy Schneeberg mountains, this water then to be heated in the hot boiler-belly and dispensed, warmly exhaled, on to the brother's learned back, to refresh him. Or on the boyish bodies of her nephews; she thinks less specifically about her sister-in-law. Nor does she see the world in neatly carved symbols, near-calligraphic emblems in the humanist tradition, sleight-of-hand presentations by later historians: lives of medieval emperors and saints fitted out in the toga-styles of Suetonius' pagan times. Of course Aunt Esterl never attended grammar school with a lot of young louts pounding out hexameters. Nevertheless, she sees the heraldic significance of the bathroom; but she cannot supply the appropriate heroic interpretation when it comes to the servants' rooms. (*Kabinetts*, as they call them in Viennese jargon.)

Here, dear sixth-formers, you behold Pure Matter. The Matter and the Spirit—the great problem seen from a new angle. Compared with the rooms beyond the bathroom region, here is an example of material at its rawest: unplaned, splintery, softwood floorboards, like base rock under mineral-rich soil—that exists, of course, in the master's drawing-room and dining-room, too, as a substratum beneath the honey-gleaming pattern of hardwood parquet; this rose-red featherbed cover is over there too, but over there it is concealed under crocheted, knotted, open-work, ribbed white ornamental covers. The life force arises from simple forms, ascending through evolutionary cycles in the course of thousands of millions of years. Nature required fifty million years to transform the terrier-sized, four-toed ancestral horse living in tropical swamp-forests into the four species of wild horse surviving today.

Thus the life force rises from rose-red basic materials of cooks' featherbeds, from the softwood splinters of the servants' chamber floor, spirals up to the shadeless electric light bulb, disperses among the complex plumbing of the Ringstrasse mansion, to rematerialise beyond the bathroom barrier in the shape of mirror-polished parquet flooring, or as crocheted, knotted, drawn-thread, ribbed white material, or, higher still, as a façade-caryatid, or plaster-white statue of Pallas Athene turning her back on the Parliament building. Finally its flight overleaps the boundary between inanimate and animate nature, to become an Imperial and High Court Advocate, or a college professor and classical philologist, *gutta cavat lapidem,* or a Member of Parliament, a minister without portfolio, Prime Minister with consequent ennoblement in perpetuity. Well, sixth-formers, do you see all that?

But all these pictures of saints have, alas, no counterpart in the honey-yellow-polished other world beyond the bathroom barrier. Saint Nepomuk (weathered green from always standing on bridges) with three stars in his hair; Leopold, sainted father of his country, on cheap paper; this whole world of pilgrims' postcards, from Maria-Drei-Eichen and Maria Taferl, the glass rosary, the thick glass globe containing crib and Child (shake the glass globe, and a snowstorm descends on the Holy Family). A servant's devotional shrine without pilgrim tourist trade. Not like the magnificent treasure house of Maria Zell—it's all rather superior there—all donated by high-minded, aristocratic old souls. A last lock of hair, tied with blue ribbon, in the consecrated glass eye of a silver medallion—for all eternity the pilgrim image of Nikolaus, Count Palffy of Erdöd, who died at the age of six. A tiny gold miner's pick on a red velvet cushion: eternal pilgrim light of the last squire of Trisana, vineyard-owner and mineralogist, from Kaltern near Meran. For ever and ever, amen, and at the hour of his death, amen. An iron rib—thanks-offering for restored health; oak twigs of gold, the acorn containing the lead bullet fired on 9th August, 1832, at King Ferdinand, later Emperor of Austria, by an assassin—thanks-offering donated by the Empress. The flight into Egypt in bronze, silver-gilt —donated by Anton Haischwang, filigree-worker, of Vienna, in 1896. The present Emperor, too, no longer shining white with youth like the white porcelain bust in the drawing-room, could do with a pilgrim's grace: here you see him as supreme war-lord, among the cockatoo plumes of his generals on a gently rounded observation mound, a dainty, ramrod-stiff figure, all benevolence yet master of the situation—a brown army postcard transfixed with a drawing-pin, *Best regards from Your Karl.* A decent journeyman carpenter, he didn't want to go to war; on the first advance march he lay down in the fresh Russian snow until the Medical Corps caught up, but the pneumonia he contracted proved fatal. So he never saw the Volga, nor even the Danube again.

Dare one linger in these dangerous servants' rooms? So far it's still the good icons that hang here, His Apostolic Majesty, and a picture postcard of the sooty, miracle-working Virgin of Maria Zell, and the clumsy signature of the honest carpenter Karl—but the best of cooks can give birth to socialist sons, red rebels without Sunday-bests. They can learn to read from mother's cookery book, certainly—Soup with Liver Dumplings:

'Scrape the skin off a goose liver and chop it finely; cream two ounces of butter or beef dripping until fluffy, add gradually two beaten whole eggs and two yolks; remove the crusts from two rolls, soak them in milk and add to the mixture, with a little chopped green parsley, salt, freshly ground pepper and breadcrumbs; stir and mix well. . . .'

Indeed. But one can go on and satisfy the appetite for reading in the Workers' Educational Library, or even attend evening classes and ask questions in the time kindly put at one's disposal, as for instance whether the proposition advanced by the clergy and taught to children, that Adam and Eve were the first human beings, was based on fact. Is it only a myth, then, that the Himalayas should be regarded as the cradle of humanity? Or even, like a certain enthusiastic trunk-maker's apprentice, refer to Science as his supreme heavenly mistress. That goes quite beyond the status of a gentile cook in a Jewish lawyer's household —it is a sacrilegious hunger which will not be appeased, be it by leg of lamb venison-style, or pigs' ears with Parmesan cheese.

Perhaps it would be better to turn back towards the frontier of the better class people, towards the courtyard, where the nursery marks the siting of hope for the future. A light room, ruled by the nanny, who is a devotee of the healthy life: on country holidays one must walk barefoot in the dew, in town the windows are kept open even at night. Snowy air, rainy air, November air, blows on the sleeping boys and blasts out evil desires—like being Old Shatterhand or Winnetou the Warrior and shooting an Indian arrow through the Latin master's black Benedictine habit, straight to the heart (which has no feeling for anything save Latin declensions). The steel beds are set far apart, the boys are to sleep quietly, no pillow-fights or wrestling in bed; a red coconut mat runs like the Red Sea between the beds. Two desks by the window, school satchels leaning against the desk legs. A long rectangular table in the dark corner by the door, an old billiard-table with a tattered green baize cover, Wild West books by Karl May and a butterfly net, straw sun-hats, an old cigar box full of stamps, a copper-shiny microscope (hairs look like ropes, thick and thin are relative terms, one single hair, quickly interpose the ground glass and it's a rope—it's a philosopher, this microscope, really), a botanical collecting tin, bourgeois butterfly coffin (you really ought to clear up some time), two cupboards—narrow-chested, space-saving, old-fashioned cupboards—shouldn't be that hard to keep tidy, the nanny tells the grammar-school boys. She is still in residence, but soon there will be a tutor instead.

Those two boys in sailor suits! Romantic dreams of the salt sea spray, ahoy, as the boys, sans governess, play ball after school on the grass of the public gardens (which you are supposed to keep off), beside rose trees neatly tied up with raffia, while the Sunday-best hangs in the cupboards: knee-breeches, blouse-like jackets and waistcoats, trappings of the good little boy. In illustrations to fat books of hobbies every such lad in knee-length sailor suit flies his kite with faultless decorum, with his fretsaw produces a cigar box for his stern but just father (later it can be used as a pencil case), doffs his sailor cap politely to teacher, vicar or other members of the Establishment, like his father and mother. They in turn watch conscientiously for these marks of filial respect, as well as over the Crown-decreed spartan austerity of the children's room. Archdukes and landed gentry, bishops- and archbishops-to-be, all suffer this privation in childhood—and quite right, too. Anyone can rise to be a bishop, even a boy circumcised in accordance with ancient rites, and well his parents know it. The Spartan nursery is the farthest outpost of all the deliberately occupied strong positions—and herewith some last-minute points to note regarding the standing orders for the ascent.

It will become necessary at some point to abandon this position and advance, from the nursery position into the very heart of the upper and uppermost castes, the powers that be in the multiracial Empire, where decorations and posts, throne and altar, landed estates and ultimately even the *'von'*, a first modest aristocratic title, can be gained. But the way does not lie over the imitation Persian rugs of the dining-room and drawing-room, nor through the master bedroom filled with dreams of a furious Solomon, nor even via the pips on the collar of the Imperial Naval Commodore. Beside the open window of their nursery outpost—that fresh air blows in straight from the Danube Canal—two sailor boys with butterfly nets and plant tin await the signal to advance. That Makart beauty of a mother and that bearded High Court Advocate with his cane on his arm, their orders are no different from those of the army captain, harshly commanding his troop in front of every war memorial : *On your knees for prayers!*

The daily walk from the Schottenring, which has nothing at all to do with Scots, much less with rings or jewels, to the Benedictine College on the left through the round dark archway beside the Schotten Church, is the beginning of the advance. And the army captain's order is also an order to carry on thus :

> The time of striking camp is to be fixed such that the column shall reach the objective of the march in good

time, if possible before dark and without undue exhaustion.

Thus it is written in the standing orders of the Imperial Army.

2 Suburb (Second Premises)

Do workers have homes? Houses? Dwellings? Dens? Doss-houses? Refuges? One room? Two rooms? No room at all? Do they live and sleep, diligent, faithful and true, in their employers' houses, like the Emperor's coachman or the Prince's stokers at His Grace's Schloss Eisgrub in Moravia? Should middle-class boys in sailor suits on Schottenring balconies train their home-made telescopes of shining brass south-east towards Favoriten and say, Papa, please look through our telescope, we want to show you a New Star, which serves for workers' socials and political meetings, but also for residential use?

That is just the sort of absurd thing our good little boy in a sailor suit will be made to say when it becomes possible to write a *Hobby Book of Twentieth Century Politics.* A model boy in a sailor suit will be pointing solemnly to the chains and padlocks of the suffragettes. He will draw painstaking diagrams of the anarchists' sooty little bombs, and trace the outline of the stiletto on which Elisabeth of Austria was impaled. A special folder of the brown briefcase filled with dynamite which, unfortunately, did not explode with sufficient force on 20th July, 1944,* will be enclosed. As a boy scout he will be prepared to blaze a trail through bacteria-infected forests looking for atomic mushrooms, genus *Hiroshima Mon Amour.* Instructions for this educational ramble will be found in the manual. They will turn our good little boy into a political hell-raising Struwwel-

* The date of the unsuccessful attempt on the life of Adolf Hitler.

peter of this our Century of the Child. Instead of overgrown finger-nails he'll have hypodermics filled with poison on his fingers: a jab for every minority—a jab for every nigger, a jab for every Jew, a jab for every Pole—jab, jab, jab, jab again!

And the workers, Papa, as those boys looking south-eastwards through their telescope from the Schottenring might ask, are they a minority too, or are they just a majority with minority rights? They certainly aren't a minority with majority rights, like the products of the Theresian Academy for Sons of Noblemen at the former Imperial country seat Favorita—dress swords scraping marble floors, avenue of poplars, creaking of carriages and obsequious letting down of carriage steps, and the chaplain of the country seat kissing the ladies' hands. And all the pleasures of sport as well, partridges and snipe tumbling gorily into the carp pond, as though in time to a famous jingle about the habits of snipe and the Sundays in Lent:

oculi, snipe I spy
laetare, here they are
judica, they won't get far
palmarum, all snipe gone!

Is Schmölzer the turner aware that the name of the district derives from the Imperial hunting lodge? Every Friday and Saturday evening he passes by like a cloth-capped Angel of the Annunciation, collecting contributions to the Fighting Fund of the Austrian Labour Party: bricks for workers' homes, pennies from heaven (better than that, proper currency gulden) towards the New Star, also new members for the Workers' Educational Institute. In return Schmölzer hands out membership stamps to the comrades, and special 'brick' stamps for donations. All these get stuck in little coloured notebooks, membership cards, Schmölzer's little catechisms that mean more to him than the great red Bible of a certain Karl M., sometime deceased in London, which embodies the Ten Commandments of the movement. He knows all about that, of course, being head of the local organisation, Angel of the Annunciation in a cloth cap, the speaker at meetings who stands up on bar-room tables to ask menacingly: Do workers have homes? Houses? Dwellings? Dens? Doss-houses? Refuges? One room? Two rooms? How do they live and sleep?

Now I, Schmölzer, am housed as every comrade shall be housed in future, every comrade who contributes to our victory, every comrade who understands the issues! I live on our New Star! You won't find any landlords there, comrades collected for the house, comrades had it built, the *Neue Stern** belongs to us! I collect my own rent! You won't find a downtrodden caretaker listening with landlord's ears to what's going on, who's saying what, trying to trap us. That's all finished! This is positively the first guaranteed classless star.

Watch Schmölzer mounting from level to level on his New Star to reach his own flat, sweeping first through the taproom on the ground floor, where the beer spurts over the counter—especially towards the weekend, on payday Friday—to be wiped up from time to time by the publican in shirt-sleeves, with a red-checked teacloth. Friendships rising out of beer-mugs in the taproom on the ground floor acquire a political meaning when they reach the first floor, take fire in the assembly hall (which holds 3,000 people) from whatever comrade is addressing the meeting with:

* Literally 'New Star', a suitably high-sounding name for workers' housing estates, planned and run on a non-profit basis.

Friendship! and (only verbally for the moment, but with no less conviction) overthrow the old order of Old Prohaska, wise, bewhiskered old Emperor and pettiest of domestic bureaucrats, together with all his beer barons (who do, however, supply the barrels and bottles for the beer-mug friendships on the ground floor, and make a profit from the contents).

Friendship is his invariable greeting, except, on the floor above, *Servus, Toni!*, when he meets his neighbour from the next door flat on the stairs, as he turns left at the bulging sink with its communal tap on the landing, to the brown front door of his own apartment, bearing the brass name-plate SCHMÖLZER. It would be easy enough to sneak in with Schmölzer through that door—first dutifully wiping one's feet—to sniff around his home, chat him up, run a sly finger over the wood of the kitchen table and the conjugal beds, like a housewife testing for dust, and find out how Schmölzer reached this position; but then, I am not in any way related to Schmölzer. His next door neighbour is another matter. Pumped through an intermediary, that blood will eventually settle in my veins; his eye colour will, according to the Mendelian laws of inheritance, have some relevance to that of my own iris; I cannot feel indifferent to the kind of beds he puts up in his one-room flat, or why he should pointedly avoid the taprooms on the ground floor, while Schmölzer positively flaunts his way through them, crying *Friendship*. Even the clothes-stand in the tiny box of a hall interests me: there are rucksacks on it, raincoats, a polished hazel wand promoted to walking-stick, a tin field bottle in grey felt cover, and in the very corner stacks of magazines—back numbers of *The Teetotaller*, monthly of the Workers' Temperance Association. One more door to that box-sized hall, a door with a panel of frosted glass, a white-painted wooden door that opens with a creak of hinges.

It opens into the kitchen. A black gas cooker with white stovepipe cover, a dresser with white starched frills edging the shelves, blue and red embroidered Dutchmen skate across this linen dyke towards the edges of the border, a kitchen table covered with blue-checked oilcloth, three white kitchen chairs, a bench by the wall with bed-linen concealed in its interior—a bed is made up on it at night for the grandfather; a kitchen table lamp with blue glass shade which can be moved up and down on a double chain by means of a weight; on the wall above the bed-bench, the annual calendar from His Imperial Majesty's Stationery Office, A Treasury of Views from the Empire, reproduced by offset process, copper engraving or lithography. January: Charles Bridge, Prague, in the snow; February: Christmas roses on the Rax; March: Budapest Castle seen from the Danube, with blossoming trees; April: the Clock Tower at Riva, on Lake Garda; through August—month of the Emperor's birthday—country estate with gamekeeper, in the Salzkammergut; on to December, church domes in Salzburg, powdered with snow and shining in the wintry moonlight, the very spirit of Advent. Employees and typesetters of His Imperial Majesty's Stationery Office get this calendar presented gratis with their Christmas bonus. The next door neighbour took home two calendars with A Treasury of Views from the Empire—that multinational Empire where everything is beginning to organise itself, into nations, into classes, into religious (or perhaps to *dis*organise itself, as the university lecturers would remark a generation later, with forefingers raised), it's not only Schmölzer and his neighbour who are getting organised on their Star—so he gave one of the calendars to Schmölzer. That is why the same calendar hangs in both kitchens. The kitchens themselves are very similar, with one exception : when the neighbour opens the second door, leading from the kitchen to the bedroom, one can see a long, narrow bookcase. Schmölzer, of course, sets more store by those little catechisms of the movement; as aforesaid, fully paid-up membership cards.

But the man next door loves his altar of books. Here are the classics, bound in red with gilt edges, in the middle the works of Karl M., the special Jubilee souvenir publication of His Imperial Majesty's Stationery Office where the neighbour spends his days working as a linotype setter in black overalls, setting up Imperial decrees and regulations for Customs offices, military hospitals, delousing centres, penal institutions, telegraph offices, mountain railway passengers and for companies of soldiers crossing bridges. The command to abandon marching pace must be given 100 metres before the bridge is reached, so that the transition to normal walking pace may be smoothly effected, crossing the bridge in marching formation could result in its collapse and is therefore an offence. In short, all day he puts letters together to form words, which then coalesce like crystals into sentences, which in turn form larger crystals of regulations and statutes, which arrange themselves into chains of gleaming crystals, which illuminate institutions, ministries, cadet training colleges, homes for deaf mutes, young ladies' seminaries for officers' daughters, and State railway stations of the Great Empire, where everything is beginning to get organised (or *dis*organised, as the university lecturers will say a generation later, with raised index fingers)—at least, as regards nationality, class and religion. These are the veritable jewels (though, chemically speaking, only paper) of national politics, and the Koh-i-noor of that wise old paternalist morality is the

Civil Code of the Austrian Empire, as amended in the light of recent legislation.

However, periodicals like *The Teetotaller*—organ of the Workers' Temperance Association—or the Neighbour's pamphlet against excessive alcohol consumption among building workers, *The thinking worker does not drink, the drinking worker does not think*, are not set up on the machines of His Imperial Majesty's Stationery Office, where only the most loyal of letters stand to attention in the printing frames. Any more than the political discussions of the inhabitants of the *Neue Stern* take place within the panelled, silk-covered walls of the white-pillared Ringstrasse Parliament, site of Most Graciously tolerated opposition; they take place, rather, in the kitchens of Schmölzer and his Neighbour. Here it is not a question of minor, Graciously sanctioned evolutionary advances like determining the exact date when a Court Cook (female) must hand over her dominion to a Court Chef (male), or the significance of the day when the first 'Supreme Chef' of the Imperial kitchen was officially appointed in the Hofburg's *Schweizertrakt*—no indeed, between the mince and the red cabbage at Sunday lunchtime, or between eight and ten at night on weekdays, after Knackwurst with oil and vinegar,* and a glass of apple juice or milk (Schmölzer would have liked a beer, but he suppressed this desire in his teetotal Neighbour's kitchen): here, at such times, His Whiskers the Emperor is finally deposed; the building foremen, those capitalist tools whose mistresses—known as 'chambermaids' —run the inferior building site canteens at the foremen's expense, are finally persuaded to join the union; skinny apprentices are ennobled from mere bed-users to full-scale

* Most popular Viennese plebeian supper dish, comparable perhaps to 'bangers and mash'.

lodgers; coming hat in hand to receive one's wages is done away with, a custom fit only for slaves and serfs.

These kitchens of the *Neue Stern* : smelling of cabbage, the table covered with oilcloth, skating Dutchmen on the shelf-edging, blue-glass lit—Schmölzer often sits at table in his ankle-length underpants in order to save the trousers of his suit, as he reads the party newspaper—it was these long rectangular kitchens, with blue-patterned friezes running below the ceiling, that cooked up the whole revolution.

Has no one ever noticed that smells can change their political significance? A smell of burning can signify the sacking of towns or monasteries (Saint Florian the Holy Fireman, help the old master of Schloss Eisgrub in Moravia : Swedes in the castle, Turks in the countryside, randy Lutherans invade the convent, set fire to the leaflets, down with everything, always that smell of burning and always a different pretext). A smell of gas can mean Death to all moths, cockroaches and bugs, but also . . . I will leave it unsaid—the History of Gas in Our Time is a thesis for theologians. A smell of cabbage can evoke grandfather on his bed-bench, wife and husband and two children in a working man's kitchen. But then again, a smell of cabbage in palaces—our victory, cabbage smell sweeping along the walls, nestling in the cool forest-green rep of the period sofas in front of some picture with a Temple of Love and a faun, cabbage smell lying thick as yellow English November fog, penetrating the barrels of shotguns and rifles; even between the uncut pages of a dredged-up chronicle of some archducal house—*hortensio pallavicino, Austriaci caesares mariae annae austriacae potentissimae hispaniarum reginae in dotale auspicium exhibiti, Milan, 1. montia, 1649*—its pervasive influence can be felt. Smell of cabbage, kitchen smell, proletarian kitchen smell. Here at the source of that smell the money for the Fighting Fund is paid out over the table, 'brick' stamps for a new *Neue Stern* accepted in return, then the *Daily Worker* is spread out—and Schmölzer and his Neighbour read the case history of Frau Michel:

> Our landlady and her three adolescent children live in the room next door. Her husband and a grown-up daughter died of tuberculosis a few years ago, her married son also suffered from the disease and died of it while I was lodging with his mother. Frau Michel, that was my landlady's name, lived wretchedly with her three children on the rents paid by her lodgers, plus a little needlework and the sparse earnings of her children, the two boys apprentices and the girl working as a domestic help. She was constantly tormented by the fear that the three surviving children would fall victims to tuberculosis. Unfortunately her fears were justified. She outlived all her children.

The story of Frau Michel is like the Gospels to Schmölzer and his neighbour; a smell of cabbage in the palaces, the appropriate incense. Schmölzer could quote the prophet Jeremiah, were he a Protestant like his Neighbour, Protestants being so well up in the Bible—but the Neighbour has no Bible on his bedside table either. Throne and Altar, the Divine Right of Kings, *cuius regio eius religio.* Don't fall for all that, say the party leaders. Anyway, who needs Jeremiah to cry out for him: 'But if ye will not hear these words, I swear by myself, saith the Lord, that this house shall become a desolation.'

When the Neighbour glances through the open kitchen door at the narrow-chested bookcase in the bedroom, the printing worker's altar of books, his thoughts do not take this prophetic turn. Instead he thinks: Where could I put a second book-altar? This one is crammed full, and there is no room for another. The Neighbour's wife, however, who before marriage was a salesgirl in the Worker's Co-operative, the non-profit-making community general store, is quite satisfied with just one bookcase in her bedroom. One domestic altar will do, as far as she is concerned. On Sunday afternoons the glass doors of the bookcase are opened, the kitchen table with its freshly starched tablecloth set in front, a glass water-jug and tumblers on it (this is a teetotal worker's home), and a few pastries. The Neighbour, Schmölzer, and another comrade sit down; their wives join them. The Neighbour takes a red classic with gilt edges from the opened bookcase, opens it and begins to read aloud:

> '. . . When evening fell on the day that Prince Wratislaw's men had been driven back through the trees of the forest, the forest dwellers reached the hill Duke Wladislaw had designated for their night encampment.
>
> They spread out over the hill and sought out suitable resting-places.
>
> Witiko summoned Sigfrid von Milnet and said to him: "Sigfrid, are you so spent with battle that you could not perform another feat tonight, and could your horse yet last out a fair ride of several hours' duration?" '

Kitchen table and bookcase represent throne and altar respectively, everything else is accessory. But, of course, the high dark-brown beds carved in pseudo-Gothic style, with twisted knobs, high piled mounds of bedclothes, embroidered bedspread with entwined monogram, have their importance too. Here the typesetter sleeps peacefully to refresh himself for the election campaign, to inveigh with a clear head against alcohol, that enemy of the working class. Here the two children were begotten. How far can procreation be considered a political act? Children are said to belong to God, or the Church, or the Army—they are soldiers for our Emperor—or to the school, the nation, the community: an insoluble legal problem of property, a Gordian knot of Common Law rights; as for that certain feeling in one's loins which accompanies procreation, to whom does that belong?

And above the beds, a picture in a gilt frame: St John the Baptist, perhaps? Or God the Father Himself, with forefinger raised? The Holy Family resting on the Flight into Egypt? Bearded Karl M. was not so common a worker's icon in those days. No, it's Dürer's *Madonna with a Pear*, that very popular picture in the Hofmuseum by the Ring, in true-colour reproduction. The two bedside tables with red-veined marble tops watch over the bed-square like temple guardians; opposite the window, a linen and clothes wardrobe with fragrant lavender sachets dangling, next to that the above-mentioned 'Learning Liberates' bookcase, and in front of the beds a low divan with round rosette-bordered seat cushions, whose tondo-shaped centres support the bottoms sitting upon them with picture stories of coloured embroidery—the one on the left shows a windmill, a canal with a boat in the foreground and a fisherman angling from it. What with skaters in the kitchen and embroidered windmill here in the bedroom, can there be some Dutch ancestors?

But why the hell should a young working-class couple not simply enjoy the *style hollandais*? Is it reserved for fat beer-barons in Ringstrasse palaces to hang dark tavern interiors with farting, puking, sodden peasant louts from the land between Maas and Schelde on their gold-papered walls? The tondo picture on the right-hand seat cushion, a Chinese reed landscape with a triangular flight formation of wild geese, does not signify anything special either. Except, perhaps, eternal longing—but that, too, is obliterated when you sit on it.

In the evening a bed is made up on this divan. This is where the younger child, the boy, sleeps. The girl sleeps in the *kabinett* adjoining the bedroom; the brass bed leaves a narrow space through which she can just squeeze her way to the desk under the window, where she does her homework. Then there is a cupboard, painted white, and an armchair by the bedhead which is put beside the bed at night with the alarm clock on it, an armchair promoted to bedside table. A spartan set-up, a room of contemporary youth, the window open at night. Live a plain and simple life, open-necked shirt for young men, linen blouse for girls, sandals, look people straight in the eye, the Youth Movement, no alcohol or nicotine, a firm handclasp. But seen in historical perspective, in the macro- and microcosm of the capital and metropolis of the multiracial Empire, the *kabinett* is a long-standing tradition unconnected with all this newfangled nonsense. The *kabinett,* a long narrow room like a hosepipe with one window, is usually—though not in this case—an isthmus rented out by impoverished landowners. I mean, a *kabinett* is usually inhabited by a furnished tenant, a lodger, a subtenant; a newcomer who has to find somewhere to sleep will indulge his alien ways there, in the evenings guzzle sausage out of greasy wrapping paper and break up a roll to go with it, smuggle in a woman now and then when the landlords are asleep, feel pretty scared though when the bed creaks, almost regret that certain feeling in his loins, because his rent is already three months' overdue. That is what you'd expect in a *kabinett.* Here on the *Neue Stern* there is usually somebody, a somebody who is a nobody, living in the *kabinett.* But when Schmölzer tried to introduce someone as a lodger for the Neighbour's *kabinett,* the Neighbour declined : I don't want to let, I prefer to save. My daughter will sleep in the *kabinett.* However, the other honeycombs of the *Neue Stern* harbour many of these rent-paying, sausage-eating drones in the *kabinett*-burrow.

Otherwise the honeycombs are all very similar. Residential honeycombs where Schmölzer, his Neighbour and their comrades store the political honey they bring back from their flying visits to the Bohemian tile-makers, the barefoot migrant workers who speak hardly any German and who sleep at night on the brick kilns—having no better quarters; bring back, too, from conferences of the Temperance Movement, woodmen's meetings in Styria, pep talks for strike pickets in the wool mills beyond the Thaya; their swarming even takes them to the Silesian textile workers—getting the honey to store in their honeycombs until the day the palaces smell of cabbage. Then at last the honey will be spread on the daily bread of party politics, then there will be honey for breakfast, breakfast and elevenses will be honey-breakfast—and this honey will have the sharp, spicy scent of red carnations.*

Don't accuse me of prudishness : I am no Queen Victoria, for whose sake the word 'leg' had to be cut from fashion descriptions; I don't call underpants 'unmentionables'. You will notice, however, that I have not yet mentioned the way of all refuse, excrement, bottle tops, screwed-up party newspapers and pamphlets, in short the way to the lavatory.

* The red carnation was the floral emblem of the Austrian Labour Party.

You have to leave the residential honeycomb for that, out on to the cold stone-flagged landing, have your key ready, and advance on the brown door of the landing lavatory, which is also used by Schmölzer's family and two others. At these times does Schmölzer ponder such subjects as brotherhood on the *Neue Stern*, each for each, and one for all, and all for one, and all for all? The hall lavatory used by Schmölzer and his Neighbour and two other families, all with children, is not actually the first and best place one would select for the glorious dawn of community feelings.

The communal sink on the landing is another matter. There the women can discuss the price of milk while the water runs into the jug, talk of having children or not having them, of wage and food wars, later on about the Great War, of wages taken home and wages that stay down in the taproom—*the thinking worker does not drink, the drinking worker does not think,* they don't put it in the form of this motto, but that's what they mean.

Standing here in a semicircle round the landing tap, during the last year but one of the Great War, the women set to demolishing the new Empress Zita, verbally that is. She is for ever driving past the *Neue Stern,* always driving with her little Imperial children past the Laxenburger Strasse to the Imperial country seat at Laxenburg, so this Italian woman, unpopular round here, has herself driven in the hunting carriage to the old hunting lodge grounds of the former dukes of Austria—rattling along in the closed, black-lacquered Imperial carriage through a strange public scrutiny.

Opposite the workers' flats, the old-style Viennese mansion of the butcher Steffl: a black sign going the whole length of the frontage, with gold letters saying STEFFL THE BUTCHER. The famous local butcher's shop of the district, with a great display window in which a pig's head can be seen growing out of a block of white marble. Steffl is a Christian Democrat, a worshipper of his party boss Lueger, one of the few Christian bulwarks against the red tide which is sweeping this district. The pig's head on the marble block has a slice of lemon and a sprig of parsley in its mouth and its eyes are closed, possibly to shut out the sinister building across the road whose skylights may sprout red flags at any moment, or possibly in prayer. On the right, the threat of red flags on the rooftops; to the left, the pig's head monument, though politically these directions are reversed. And the Empress of Austria passes by and has no idea what the women in the block on the right are saying about her.

There goes that damn Zita again! We have to wrap our kids in paper nappies, wartime nappies, but she's still got the very best, softest peacetime nappies for her Hapsburg brats. . . .

But what do the nattering women expect? Should this young mother, born of the House of Bourbon-Parma, refuse to be driven to Schloss Laxenburg? Should she, to please the women, drive instead to the Laar-Berg, refuse dump of the City of Vienna—every year the Municipality of Vienna produces 300,000 cubic metres of domestic refuse, $\frac{1}{4}$ cubic metre per head, 1 cubic metre weighing approximately 500 kilograms—perhaps even poke about in the steaming rubbish pit with the old hags for something usable, and pay the municipality of Vienna for the privilege? After they have finished their sifting, the unusable remains serve to feed the rats, or in the end simply rot, producing a most frightful stench. What is it the gossiping women want? Oh, those daydreams of the revolutionary women, fantasies of humiliating the Empress Zita, they keep one going!

To descend from the topic of conversation at the sink, one or two storeys down into the assembly hall that holds 3,000—enter and take part in an election meeting, a protest meeting, a people's rally—nothing could be easier. The conversations round the sink and the speeches at meetings are ruled by the same star. When Schmölzer opens a meeting and introduces the speaker, when the latter raises his voice to say, the Union demands not merely a daily wage of four kronen, but also that every building site should have a building site hut, a room where the workers can keep their tools and outdoor clothes—indeed, more than that, these huts should have benches and tables, just raw planks nailed together—then Frau Schmölzer, while fetching water, can add the final touch, she tells the women that this hut ought to have a lock on the door; but perhaps that's really asking too much!

There are other kinds of festivities in the hall, too. The rows of tip-up seats are removed, the floor is waxed, the hall doors get washed and the stage—no platform, no political chancel now—on the stage the 'Free Typography', amateur band of the Printers' Union, is playing. A carnival ball, its theme—'Orange Ball'—thought up by the Neighbour and approved by Schmölzer and presumably by the other inhabitants of the *Neue Stern*. The band sits in an orange grove, hundreds of oranges dangle above the hall, which can hold 3,000 seated and considerably more than that dancing, and—the Neighbour's supreme triumph—orange juice is the only drink. Not a bottle of wine, not a mug of beer passes the threshold. The Worker's Temperance Association is proving that it can have a good time without wine or beer, solely on orange juice. The dancing couples here on the parquet (not too fearfully plebeian, doesn't actually look all that revolting, as an Imperial Army brigadier might say, should he happen to come this way), those printers, carpenters, mechanics, this workers' aristocracy of skilled men, black-suited with carnations in their button-holes, wives in ballgowns : true, it hasn't the verve, the certain something of the laundry girls' ball, the People as they live and breathe and as the fine gentlemen, the brigadier and his dear old pals, love to see them—it's not like that. A conscious dignity, decently restrained waltzing, that's what marks a ball on the *Neue Stern.*

But it's also a kind of ball (without music, to be sure) when palaces tumble, the multiracial Empire at last breaks up into its several component nations, the above-mentioned cabbage smell blows strongly in the desired direction, and the Neighbour mounts the sill in front of his kitchen window —Schmölzer holding on to the back of his jacket—and calls to the crowd standing down there in front of the *Neue Stern,* expecting something or other, he calls to the loyal party rank and file of his electoral district (doubtless there were violinists, pipers and drummers of the 'Free Typography' among them) : 'Long live the Republic !' Rejoice, ye masses !

Everyone knows that roar of an excited crowd, which turns into a crocodile, beating its tail on the hard pavement of the working-class district, causing the old Imperial crowns in the Hofburg treasure vaults to tremble. A giant crocodile, now throwing open its huge jaws for the first time in overt, forceful political action, showing the red throat of the Republic. Republics also need a heraldic beast : why not a crocodile? Is a crocodile any worse than an (unfortunately now only single-headed) eagle? Perhaps the latter will one day long for the second head of its predecessor.

What is happening to things inside the apartment while the Neighbour is standing on the kitchen window-sill and the people's crocodile is gulping in the air of its new freedom? Schmölzer is still holding the back of his coat, and he is still calling down, again and again: Long live the Republic! The contents of the apartment are reborn, like those two revolutionaries Schmölzer and his Neighbour, like the comrades in the crowd outside the house. Soon they are due to be moved from the *Neue Stern* to the *Neueste Stern*,* a few things will get lost on the way, others will be set up in new positions; in short, the declaration of the Republic and the Neighbour's move from the *Neue* to the *Neueste Stern*, both see old things put into a new order.

But the fire, which burns so brightly on the *Neue Stern* towards the dawn of a beautiful future of classless happiness, will that survive transplanting? The forces of righteousness were just getting so well into their stride, and the Neighbour's son and daughter know when they catch sight of red-bearded Professor Smola, who is at once head, spirit and heart of the Clothing Reform Movement (corsets! belts! waistcoats! cummerbunds! moustache-trainers! lace-up shoes! neckties—burn the lot!), that the path to the dawning of a new age can only be trodden in strapless sandals, with Professor Smola going on before.

The two children watch worker-athletes in red leotards whose parades give the petty bourgeoisie of the area a proper goosefleshy terror of the future; their emergence is greeted with sour glances and Christian swear-words, this sinister gladiators' world of muscle-men wrapped in red contrasting with the troops of innocent children clad in white. Candles in hands they follow in the Corpus Christi procession, behind the gold-embroidered swaying canopy, sing pious

* Literally 'Newest Star', the even more progressive workers' housing estate, municipally planned and run, built with ratepayers' money.

hymns, their glances bent to the ground, perpetually conscious of their guilt.

The worker-athletes, on the other hand, look up at the sky, although they can't expect much help from there, and they too have their songs, home-made at that, and not coached by an incense-scented choirmaster:

> 'Ropes and bars
> Do not despise
> The wicked
> Do not exercise.'

In the basement of the building are the gymnasium dance-halls, one large and one small. Every day, every hour, people exercise here—every day and every hour one must be prepared for the breakthrough into the New Age. The gym-rooms are thus like a battleship after war has been declared, permanently under steam, and the Neighbour's wife can say to her two children at any time of day 'Oh, run down and do some gym!' if they are too much under her feet in the small flat. Someone is always exercising down in the gym.

The worker-athletes have their songs, as aforesaid, but the best voices among the workers prefer to join the Workers' Glee Club. Yet the very finest, smoothest, softest voices of all belong to the famed local Treu Quartet (Comrade Alfred Treu was its prematurely deceased founder), which sings at comrades' funerals beside the open grave 'Rest in peace!' *pianissimo*, grief-extendingly and heart-rendingly. The Neighbour's daughter will remember the Quartet as funeral singers above all, although their other functions are really more important to the fame of the Treu Quartet, like rounding off party occasions, or

Sunday afternoon concerts in the theatre hall of the *Neue Stern,* singing at weddings and national song contests. But to that child running along the single rail of her development, those four singers of the Treu Quartet are simply the mourning-birds of the district. Should she chance to meet one of them walking by himself during the musicless working week under the chestnut trees of the Laxenburger Allee, even without his black suit, and not really capable of song (because the other three are missing), he is still the mourning-bird. And even on his own he might at any moment open his bill to call out 'Rest in peace!'

Everything possible is done to guard that flame: the Muses enlisted in the Class War (transported to the Front by the Workers' Glee Club, assisted by the four mourning-birds of the Treu Quartet) and in addition the People's Theatre, famous throughout Vienna, gives a performance every evening in the theatre of the *Neue Stern.* But who thanks the Director for the wide range of his repertory? His grandiose dream is to be director of the Hofburgtheater of the Suburbs, and in this dream he climbs a sort of repertory-pyramid: with *The Miller and His Child* at the bottom, then rising via *The Scribblers, The Peasant Millionaire* and *King of the Alps and Misanthropist* to *Hamlet, Wallenstein* and *Faust.* We'll do the lot! A limited repertory? Not for the Director of the People's Theatre! He sports dyed side-whiskers, is always well groomed, and does not know the meaning of the word 'limited'. True, the financial resources at his disposal, when compared with those of the Hofburgtheater—but that's a sterile comparison. . . .

The donkey, a real live donkey which appears in the popular tragedy *The Miller and His Child*, has to be brought on stage via the residential staircase. Naturally it cannot manage the stairs, planks have to be laid up the staircase, and the Neighbour's daughter looks on to see the donkey-star conquer the stairs, see him led towards the stage. From the kitchen window, beyond the light-shaft, she can see the actors sitting at their dressing-tables and transforming themselves, abracadabra, into kings or beggars. She envies her school friend Poldi who is actually allowed to act, in the part of a fairy—a pretty cheap fairy. A week before the performance Poldi is already running about with a headful of stiff curls set with sugar and water. The Neighbour himself, however, forbids his children to act as extras for the People's Theatre. What a shame, he believes in the strength-giving properties of sleep before midnight—good for grown-ups and how much more so for children.

On the one hand these puritanical rules, on the other the Neighbour himself is a capital dancer, indeed he takes a dancing class for deaf mutes in the garden-room of the workers' home. To this end he has taught himself deaf-and-dumb sign language. He tells his children about the enthusiastic deaf-mute dancers and explains to them how the sound vibrations from the band are transmitted by the wood floor, the dance music so to speak going straight to the deaf mutes' feet without passing through the labyrinth of the inner ear : fantastic dancers they are.

And all this—red-haired Professor Smola and his battalion of uncompromising Dress Reformers, the gladiator company of worker-athletes in red tights, the worker-singers, Rest in peace, the People's Theatre and the stair-climbing donkey, the waltzing deaf mutes—all this is to be left behind now, after the setting up of the Republic. The *Neue Stern* is to be replaced by the *Neueste Stern*—at least for the Neighbour and his family, and for Schmölzer too. Let us hope the fire will not be extinguished in the course of this star voyage.

Of course things don't change just like that. This is not Ronacher's Palace of Varieties, playing to an audience feverish with inflation and the end of a world—thousand-kronen notes that will just about buy a sandwich; a million for one sip of champagne; rabbits, white-eared and red-eyed, pulled out of glossy top hats by their long ears; Juanita Gomez, *née* Heuberger, sawn in half; the Indian Rope Trick; cascades of paper flowers from a buttonhole; endless cigarettes out of the ear of the gentleman in the front row—now these are what you would call real transformations, quick, colourful and hedonistic. The Indian Rope Trick is directed neither against the Old Order of the multi-racial Empire nor against the New Order of government by the people. Rabbits, white-eared and red-eyed, may spend their rabbit lives in shiny toppers and be drawn out by their ears, sponsored neither by grace of God and the Emperor nor by the new President of the State, but their swift transposition has, abracadabra, no political significance.

On the *Neue Stern*, on the other hand, every change of position is either 'a milestone on the road to ultimate victory', 'a tactical detour', or 'a retreat dictated by the enemy'. Obviously amidst all these circumstances, party conscience, responsibility to comrades, working-class unity, things cannot change their position lightly, just like that, like conjuror's rabbits. No, some really momentous change has to be enacted to bring the furniture and all the other possessions from the *Neue* to the *Neueste Stern*.

It needs something stronger than the spirit that moved, or failed to move, the caretaker at the *Neue Stern*, Herr Wustubal, in the old Hapsburg days. Wustubal always had to hang out the great red flag with its heavy staff, for May Day, for election meetings, to greet strike deputations and demonstrations—movements from all the alleys, all the streets, all the squares of the district, converging to the heart centre of the *Neue Stern*: a flawlessly functioning political blood circulation—and the Deputy, the chosen representative, stands ready to do the honours. But first Wustubal always had to drag the heavy flagstaff with its red cloth up to the attic, had to run it up, as the beautiful saying goes, run it through a narrow skylight, fix the pole in the iron hole of the flag-stand, and then on top of that fasten the lower corner of the flag with string to a nail in the wall —a red sail in a fresh breeze, which always blows from the Laar-Berg down over the Laxenburger Allee and the Favoritenstrasse, whirling up dust and cigarette stubs. The red cloth of the flag must unfurl at the right moment, that's Wustubal's responsibility, and it must not be torn by the wind—that would be symbolic of some non-event. Once the vanguard of a demonstration is already approaching, and Wustubal has not yet carried out his flag duty, the Red Flag of Revolution does not yet flutter in the breeze— the Deputy calls for the flag, he yells at Wustubal, who yells back enraged, 'One sodding red flag won't make your revolution!'—which shows that Wustubal's spirit will hardly move mountains, nor anything else very far.

That shout from the window-sill, Long live the Republic!, has no effect on the round divan cushions, on the white-painted kitchen chairs, or on the bed-bench where the grandfather has to sleep. Even the skating Dutchmen on the kitchen dresser-edging are unmoved, inanimate objects cannot be moved so easily. It is only the decision to build the *Neueste Stern*, the workers' fortress on the outskirts of the city, that will gradually change their lives.

There, near the water tower—a red-brick building adorned with spires and round turrets, with steeply rising conical roof and weathercock, terminal of the former Franz Joseph Pipeline, bringing water from the Alps, the head of water at this point amounts to approximately 33 metres. The installation consists of two Galloway boilers with two boiler pipes, each of 52 square metres effective heating surface and 8 atmospheres working pressure, as well as two steam turbines, each of 45 horse-power and two pairs of pumps coupled to the steam turbines; the district, which rises towards the south, needs a good head of water—here the foundations of the *Neueste Stern* are being excavated. No longer does Schmölzer have to walk his feet off collecting brick stamps, no statute-burdened supporters' society counts the hellers and the groschen now, laboriously scraping together building funds. The *Neueste Stern* is built out of ratepayers' money, and why should the Neighbour of Schmölzer and the other comrades, elected by free and secret ballot, be sitting in Parliament in the Ringstrasse temple building, gleaming white and gold just as in ancient Athens, if the power of the people could not say through this spokesman of Schmölzer and comrades: 'Hand over the money! We are building the *Neueste Stern*!'

Schmölzer—who has an uncomplicated view of things—tells himself, the source of our funds has acquired a new pumphouse. Well, hurray! No longer the shabby committee room or the kitchen, where comrades sit in council, but this gorgeous white pillar-adorned Parliament building on the Ring, where the Neighbour now sits as a Member, is the new Alpine Water Pipeline of wealth, honourably won in electoral battle. There, behind four cast-bronze horse-breakers standing on granite pedestals on the ramp and eight statues of historians on the ramp wall—beneath these gables bearing the gable groups of 'Justice' and 'Home Office Affairs', sheltered by eight bronze quadrigas in the corners, the latter led across the Parliament roof by winged Victories, and in front of marble niches sprouting Greek gods—the Neighbour can say more readily, more joyously: 'I formally request the necessary funds for the building of the *Neueste Stern*!' And then to Schmölzer and comrades: 'But mind you build it as a fortress!'

Later, at the official opening of the *Neueste Stern*, the 'Free Typography' band plays the 'Workers' Anthem' and Schmölzer with a red carnation in his buttonhole stands proudly in front of the speaker's rostrum while the Neighbour, the Member of Parliament, makes a speech: Healthy, dry homes for workers' families, children's playgrounds with trees and green lawns in the yards, a public bath in every apartment block, the worker having reached his majority will no longer spend his weekend in the pub, he will spend it in the public library and in the Civic Centre for Education (Learning Liberates!). But does Schmölzer know, and the loyal comrades that surround the rostrum, the crowd of new tenants, the women in freshly starched summer dresses and the children carrying red, blue and white windmills whose celluloid wheels creak in the wind, and the men and fathers, a happy crowd, almost everyone here assembled is getting a new apartment—are they aware, as they stand so proudly in the courtyard of their fortress, that fortresses attract enemies? A four-square courtyard, with arcaded flanks, a courtyard with small balconies for workers' homes, 'box balconies' in popular jargon. In the First District, for instance, the Tabriz rugs and Persian carpets of Ringstrasse apartments are beaten and hung out over their parapets. On Fridays, carpet dust clouds over the equestrian statues of the Old Town as thick as flocks of doves. Sundays are not so much ushered in by church bells as heralded by the carpet-beating on the balconies on Fridays. But here at the

Neueste Stern there are no little Tabriz rugs, not even fake Persians. So what use are the box balconies? Does Schmölzer perhaps hope to extend each box balcony into a donjon? Are the drainpipes meant to be embrasures? Where is the Enemy? Nothing but comrades all around, crying 'Friendship', singing the 'Workers' Anthem', looking forward to their new premises. They hope to keep a rabbit on the balcony, or a couple of chickens (fortunately the house-rules forbid this), keep their watering cans on it, dry the washing, look down from it at the children as they jump through hoops in the asphalt courtyard with its little squares of lawn—nevertheless, they live in fortified towers. The twelve staircases with twelve flats on each staircase—box balconies facing inwards, a plain window front to the exterior—form a battle and residential tower complex. Apparently an Enemy has yet to be found for the fortified towers of the *Neueste Stern*.

His Whiskers the Emperor died before ever the Neighbour could shout from the kitchen window-sill 'Long live the Republic!' So who the hell is the Enemy? Those brigadiers with their torn-off epaulettes and captains of Uhlans without their horses, cringing in their old class-styled apartments, are they likely to mount an attack against the *Neueste Stern*? Bring up mortars against illegal rabbits and tolerated watering cans on the box balconies? Where would they get the mortars from? Which Mounted Messenger of the former Imperial Army would deign, in his flowing horsehair-plumed helmet, to ride along the Wiedner High Street, past greengrocers, furniture stores, cobblers' vaults and bakers' shops, across Matzleinsdorfer Square and the Triester Strasse, southwards to the *Neueste Stern*, in order to return home with the report that a certain Schmölzer is standing on a box balcony with a drainpipe embrasure, turning a watering can upside-down to drain it properly! That's the trouble: it isn't always easy to find friends, but at the same time it can sometimes be quite difficult to find your enemies.

Schmölzer and his Neighbour tell themselves: We built the *Neue Stern.* Now we have erected this *Neueste Stern,* we will plant the Flag of the Republic on those two crenellated towers, red-white-red flapping to left and right, the white centre stripe like the unexplored parts of a map—perhaps one day that, too, will turn red, and then it shall be all red like the flags of the comrades east of Brest-Litovsk. The carriage-wide main gate, the portcullis with iron railings the thickness of a child's arm is permanently open, only shut at night after 10 o'clock by the caretaker who lives rent-free on the ground-floor flat of Staircase Number 1: it has to be locked then in accordance with official closing time. One could of course lock it by day too, if the Enemy did come, and twelve times twelve comrades with their families would make no mean garrison for the fortress. But who the hell is the Enemy? The disarmed field-marshal without a pension in his apartment (still in accordance with his rank), the horseless captain of Uhlans, the beer-barons with their outdated aristocratic titles, the Czechs beyond the Thaya, the priest and his petty-bourgeois confessants? The victorious comrades east of Brest-Litovsk, between the Volga and the Don, are you quite sure they are allies? And the child-loving Americans, lugging forth semolina and flour and Quaker oats, all for the starving schoolchildren of the Red Community of Vienna? They helped to reduce the population of the country from fifty to seven million, not in a lethal way to be sure, solely by means of liberation for all peoples in the former multiracial-imperial dungeon. Scrub all that. This is not an educational seminar of the

Working Men's College, where Enemy, Enmity, Class Hostility (class hostility is a political hostility, the Class War is a means to an end) can be defined, with the aid of a grammar-school master of Jewish extraction. The first task is to build the *Neueste Stern*, furnish, open and organise it. The Enemy will come all right. Should he lose his way and not take up his position in front of the two crenellated battle towers, both flying the Flag of the Republic, the local caretaker will close the wrought-iron gate, wide enough to take a carriage, peacefully; every night at 10 p.m., but never, for the present, by day, solely according to the official closing regulations.

Above all we must stick together. Together Schmölzer and his Neighbour move to the *Neueste Stern.* The Neighbour is directed to the second floor of Staircase Number 1. But a floor here has a significance that is completely different from that of the *Neue Stern*, for the two apartments on the first and second floors of Staircase Number 1 are the only honeycombs here that can claim to harbour queen bees—perhaps the metaphor is too Romantic Movement, but something is rotten in the State of Denmark, so obscure metaphors are called for.

The united front breaks down here. There are two rooms plus two *kabinetts*, a bath and water-closet; kitchen, box-room and box balcony are common to all the other flats. But this multitude of rooms! One felt guilty merely planning this queen bee suite. What has become of unity and fraternity, if two of the comrades live in four rooms apiece, while the remaining voters have to look to the future in a kitchen/living-room with one bedroom and, at best, a *kabinett*? There were arguments during the building committee meetings, Schmölzer thumped the table, the architect —an elderly gentleman—clutched his heart: But gentlemen, I beg you to reach some agreement, I have to hand in the plans—and after all, there are doctors, professional men, schoolmasters, who belong to the party too. That was the way out, the vision in answer to a prayer. The large apartments get built, and at the end of the crucial session Schmölzer says : Those are the two doctor's apartments. The other committee members quite see this : after all, a doctor needs a waiting-room, the *kabinett* would do for that, and a surgery as well.

There they are, all ready, the two doctor's apartments, and indeed a doctor of medicine, Dr Max Friedenthal, with two children and a wife, does move into the doctor's apartment on the first floor—a graduate in the Complete Course of the Medical Sciences, as the diploma has it, at the *Neueste Stern*. The second doctor's apartment goes not to a doctor but to the Neighbour, the legally elected Member of Parliament and representative of the Electoral District, in the centre of which shine the *Neue Stern* and the *Neueste Stern*, sending rays of light and joy into the Assembly, a whole galaxy of similar stars may be predicted in advance. New and ever-new stars of this species will come into being, as well as other related stars, a sea of stars, through which the comrades will steer a steady course. Provided one can ignore the fact that the Neighbour is not, in fact, a doctor, neither of Medicine, nor of Philosophy, nor of Laws, and he can hardly be a Doctor of Divinity—yet, nevertheless, he gets the doctor's apartment on the second floor.

How did that come about? Indirect bribery of the people's elected deputy, fawning recognition of the new powers that be, Schmölzer's intrigues—after all, he sits on the Homes and Buildings Committee, he can put a word in when apartments are assigned. Should I now, belatedly, demand an official investigation, an all-party Parliamentary Commission, a Party Court of Arbitration, a Pacification Committee of the Trade Union? But there has been no dispute. I just imagine that there might be one, if the elections go the other way, if the Republican crocodile is changed back to the Monarchist vulture, if the owner of the apartment loses his seat in Parliament or antagonises the Party Chairman, who is no teetotaller. But leave the scaredy-cats with those officially prohibited rabbits on the box balcony, go on, open the mirror-shiny, white-painted door on the landing with the brass spyhole and the name on the brass strip below, step into the lobby and say: 'Friendship!'

Should I enter otherwise than I used to, just because the premises are bigger? Should I act the suppliant, trying to reach the ears of the pillar-elevated Parliament, complete with gold-helmeted Pallas Athene, via this ante-room, like a war widow trembling for her pension, like an unemployable nut-case left by the war with a bullet in his brain, standing on his right to work but insisting that he be sent to a war victims' welfare convalescent home first to recuperate, like a party comrade warning you against another party comrade, like a delegate of the Printers' Union bringing an invitation to the morning reception in honour of your being made an honorary member, for whatever purpose—I don't have to employ tricks, I am a member of the family, I don't even wait in the lobby, but throw open doors to look into the rooms and find out, swiftly as a member of the secret police, what has been newly bought, what has been brought along from the *Neue Stern* to the *Neueste Stern*, how the move has affected the general situation, what has happened here.

For instance, how does a bookcase feel when it suddenly acquires a playmate? True, one can't expect bookcases to behave like sportive dolphins, leap about, chase one another—be it only through drawing- and dining-room—collide, snapping. A comparison with children playing and quarrelling also breaks down; one can carry animism too far, there are no poltergeists or spiritualist seances here, no bourgeois religious masturbation in which books, chairs, tables and other heavy objects are moved about, levitate, float down again like a maple leaf—no, the bookcase game on the *Neueste Stern* is of the most elevated kind, yet wholly of this world. It is not really the bookcases that play with each other, but the spirit of *homo ludens* seizing upon their contents. The Neighbour's daughter, Youth Movement oriented, now a grammar-school girl wearing sandals, decides to try out an intellectual game with the bookcases. So far the works of Karl M., sometime deceased in London, still stand next to the red-bound, gilt-edged classics: however, the dutiful *Trompeter von Säckingen* doesn't really go with the rebellious *Hessische Landbote*, she decides, nor do *Soll und Haben** and the *Communist Manifesto* really make a pair; the *Graphic Review*, organ of the Printers' Union, and *The Teetotal Worker*, a monthly of limited influence, could stay together at a pinch, but when it comes to literature, the self-imposed rules of the intellectual game demand absolute segregation. Every book to which she and her friends, candid, unhypocritical, wishful parricides, can say yea, is worth two such as *Der Trompeter von Säckingen, Soll und Haben* or *Der Grüne Heinrich.* In the evenings, when her parents are out and her sport-loving younger brother is already in bed, she sits swapping books around. The old Bibles—as she calls the red classics—go into the old book-altar from the *Neue Stern*; the new bookcase—which has a black-lacquered, wood-fronted abdomen, and rising above two white pillars, a glass-fronted chest—

* *Soll und Haben* = Debit and Credit.

becomes the vessel of the New Spirit. It shall hold books which can be taken out of rucksacks by camp-fires, opened and shown to friends, without shame at one's father's reactionary taste, one could read out bits to friends without spoiling the approaching dawn of the hikers' Sunday, possibly even give them away; my book, which I love, shall be your book as well, intellectual goods should not be individually owned, nor should material ones for that matter. But it will be some time before everybody has everything, before all can be all things to all men. For the moment the works of Karl M. can stay in the new bookcase, and the *Hessische Landbote* won't be weeded out either. A volume of poems by Christian Friedrich Schubart can also stay, but a volume of Mörike and Stifter's *Witiko* is relegated to the old book-altar. A Youth Movement comment beside the camp-fire: Schubart . . . eighteenth century . . . restless genius . . . had no influence . . . too far from rococo dalliance . . .

Don't wake the tormentors before their time,
For humanity's sake, don't wake them—
Oh, soon roaring above their heads will shake them,
Justice's thunder. . . .

Schubart can stay, but the bookcase game comes to no satisfactory conclusion, the old altar fills up more and more, there are few chances of exchange, the shelves of the new case remain largely empty, thirsting for knowledge, open to modern influences, but unfilled. Rilke's slim *Cornet* is no shelf-filler—the daughter bought him out of her pocket money; the bronze figure of a miner, gift of the Union's Wage Claim Committee to their secretary, swings its pick beside the supporting pillars in the middle of the bookcase

—but that doesn't help much, a pick is not a pen, the secretary of the Wage Claim Committee, the girl's father, is not interested in these games. He does not even realise that the single bookcase has got a playmate, he simply says, We have two bookcases now : there's progress for you.

Nor was it he who bought the piano. The Neighbour's wife—but the term Neighbour is out of date, as Schmölzer lives on Staircase Number 10 in a mere one-room, kitchen and *kabinett* apartment, at best a spiritual neighbour—anyway, she ordered it. The Deputy's wife, that's a better, more suitable name for her, one day took her courage in both hands and, full of trepidation though outwardly resolute, entered the famous old-established piano dealers next to the Paulan Church on Wiedner High Street, looked timidly round the Steinway grands and Bechstein monsters, middle-class aliens gleaming coldly like black ice, and chose this upright piano : payable in twenty-four monthly instalments.

There it stands, then, in the new dining/living-room at the *Neueste Stern*, the upright piano in the doctor's apartment, just as it should, with a protective cover of green baize bearing the elaborate scroll signature of the old-established piano dealers Bleibtreu & Co., embroidered in gold, over the white ivory keys, a metronome on top, gold pedals reaching out to the children like foot-traps. Treading the pedals, *per aspera ad astra*, the pair might well ask themselves where they are going. I could use a mixed metaphor and point to this upright piano as the very flypaper of ambitious cultural aspirations on the part of the Deputy's wife. Once the children, unwillingly fidgeting on the rotating piano stool, have tangled with Czerny's exercises, they will stick to this musical flypaper, their mother hopes, and, endlessly practising Czerny scales and kicking their pedal-treading childish feet, play themselves up to heights that can only be sighted from a doctor's apartment.

There is the dining-table too, a new addition to the décor, with hideous curved legs tapering towards the bottom : easily extendible, Madame, and of course you can arrange six or eight comfortably round this table for any meal, lunchtime or evening as you please (O Deputy's wife), without any extra provision whatsoever, says the able salesman.

To arrange six or eight persons round an extending dining-table, in such a way that no one elbows his neighbour at table while spooning the soup or cutting up meat, would appear a simpler task than Czerny exercises on the upright piano in the corner. But now, in this doctor's apartment at the *Neueste Stern*, to group six or eight guests so as to cause no offence, diplomacy and politics, those Siamese twins of statesmanship, will always recall that circus act with the big and small clown and a bucket of water, in between the lion-taming acts. One should be able to adopt the mocking, greyhound smile of a Metternich, like a medicament on prescription, before one tries to bring together at one table (however extendible) Schmölzer and comrades (the literary-cultural evenings are rarer now), Dr Max Friedenthal and his wife, Fräulein Dinghofer, the honorary secretary of the Workers' Temperance Association, and the hostess's mother—bring them together in spirit, that is.

Dr Friedenthal only cares to converse with Comrade Schmölzer at an extended dining-table for six to eight persons, while the normally boisterous Schmölzer with his crude orator's gestures and practised electioneering voice is suddenly silent as a fish. The hostess's mother, a German-Hungarian Protestant of peasant descent, cannot help him bridge the silence. An extendible dining-table that creates problems of assimilation for its users, a Sigmund Freudian problem—this goes well beyond the flag-wimpled battlements of the *Neueste Stern*, reaching into the courtyard, sombre with statues, of Vienna University (wall-grey, pointed arches, neo-Gothic arches)—where such problems, however, are not analysed, weighed, discussed, thought out or thought about, but rather laughed to scorn : there are still many taboos even here.

Are there in fact ways, roads, paths, tracks of any sort from the domestic fortress on the city periphery to the pillar-proud educational fortress by the Ringstrasse between Schottenring and Parliament? Could the professors in their black coats, watch-chains dangling, stiff-collar supported scholarly heads, wives of impeccable Civil Service stock, their appointments sealed by the Emperor's own hand—could they not write a new kind of guidebook, 'Rambles from the Residential Fortress to the Educational Fortress'? With ten fold-away maps in five-colour reproduction? The best rambler's path still goes by way of Caesar and Cicero, *Gallia divisa est, ceterum censeo aurea prima satast,* Virgil, Thucydides and Sophocles, theological college, Church Latin is still Latin of a sort, straight to the black-habited Inner Courtyard of the Educational Fortress, and thence without detour to the non-fencing, virtually defenceless, Catholic fraternities. A little higher up the porous educational rocks lie the upper-middle-class mountain paths of liberal humanism, but here too the wanderer will need Greek and Latin for sustenance, though without black-monkish wrapping round the sandwiches.

Dr Max Friedenthal of the second doctor's apartment has skirted the rim of this highland path; I say the rim advisedly, because he was not a moneyed student. There are, of course, in addition German national, Czech national,

Polish and Slovene national byways branching off the high-land path; the Slav national byways invariably lead—frequently via French lowlands—back to the national mountain home, and also, allegorically speaking, back to the miracle-working Black Madonna of Czenstochau.*

But the revolutionary troop with the battle-cry of 'Learning Liberates', advancing to the drumbeats of the amateur band 'Free Typography', with free, unclouded, teetotal heads (*the thinking worker doesn't drink*) and horny workers' hands, lathe-skilled, plane-habituated, hammer-strong and blowlamp-swift—horny hands that can wield not only tools but also Williamowitz-Möllendorf's *Dictionary of Classical Antiquity*, searching as a blowlamp or Diogenes' candle, nonchalantly opening the book at the word Omphalos, navel of the world: where is this ramblers' band? I wish they would do something useful, smash the plaster busts in the University Senate House (hammer-accustomed as they are) to fragments, break the sabres on the forbidden fencing floor with their bare hands, use the white, starched fraternity caps as water vessels.

But the pleasant path of popular education, lined with shelves of readily comprehensible books, frequented by the friends of workers' education who do not cry 'Thalassa!' at the cultural sea of the University Library, hardly ever leads to a doctorate, that bourgeois patent of nobility, complete with seal-stamp eye on parchment face. The little band of student revolutionaries, wearing sandals and open-necked shirts, sons of lawyers and doctors often of Jewish origin, here on the educational fencing floor of the second oldest university in German-speaking lands, can one only take it seriously as a vanguard on the educational footpath from residential to educational fortress? They themselves

* The most popular Polish shrine.

did not grow up in residential fortresses and are unconsciously ashamed of that, a queer shame at not having been born below one's actual class. Wherever I look there are problems of assimilation, be it at the extendible dining-table, where Schmölzer and the grandmother from deepest rural Burgenland have to suffer their little assimilatory purgatories, or in the University courtyard, where revolutionary sons of professional men, wearing sandals and open-necked shirts, walk up and down discussing universal questions: How can we get hold of a genuine working-class student, skilled at the lathe, plane-habituated, hammer-strong and blowlamp-swift, with genuine calluses on his hands, yet versed in Greek and Latin to the level of Omphalos, navel of the world?

Why so impatient? Why this burning desire for short cuts on the stony path to education? Here in the Neighbour's apartment—I'll go on calling him the Neighbour, though Schmölzer does live on Staircase Number 10—two healthy children are growing up, one of each sex. One day they will be your working-class students. Not for nothing has the bookcase acquired a mate, not for nothing does the new upright piano stretch out its pedals like snares for legs, whose owners, schoolchildren ceaselessly practising Czerny scales and fidgeting with small pedalling feet, work themselves up to heights which can only be sighted from a doctor's apartment.

Bookcase companions and upright piano—as cult vehicles of the Class War they beat red flags, banners for the May Day march, party cards and union news-sheets, even as the Holy Oak of Maria Taferl surpasses the less popular pilgrimage trees in Danube-watered Lower Austria. The pilgrims used to take leaves and wood shavings away with them, bits of Sacred Oak are also given away wrapped in blotting-paper, you put the wood in some water and use that for washing, or drink it, against dropsy for example, call it simply Wood Water, or even swallow an oak splinter to dislodge a fishbone. May I take the parallel further—unafraid of the fangs of the Party Court—and call Czerny's scales an Evensong for the Black Mass of class emancipation; the creaking of the bookcase door heralds the climax of the ceremony as the squeak of a tabernacle door did in former days.

The kitchen bench-bedstead, the skating Dutchmen blue and red embroidered on the linen dyke, the much-admired colour print from the former Imperial Court Museum—Dürer's *Madonna with a Pear*—the divan cushion with the windmill, the other divan cushion with the Chinese reed landscape: all these have been transferred from the *Neue Stern*. They do not stand out on the *Neueste Stern* as do the second bookcase and the upright piano and the shining brass telescope on the box balcony—a Christmas present for the sixteen-year-old son.

The stone bellies of the box balconies harbour stands for old shoes waiting to be polished. Wooden cages for pets, though the house-rules prohibit them: the rabbit eats carrots, the hen cackles to report an egg, the white mouse stinks. Often there is a tin hip-bath, washing is hung up to dry above the clean white gleaming tin bathtub.

There is good material here for a *Box Balcony Still Life*: carrot and rabbit—the white washing, the red of the carrot, the white pelt of the mouse, the red crest and wattle of the hen, light reflections on the hip-bath. But no member of the family can appreciate the ingredients of this still life, not one of them attends evening classes in art.

Nor is the telescope here for aesthetic reasons. The sixteen-year-old does not sit on the balcony in his winter coat, muffler and fur-lined mitts on clear, starry winter evenings to discover aesthetic laws: he scans the starry sky above the former Imperial capital and metropolis, now the capital of a small republic, scans the starry sky above the nearby water tower from an amateur astronomer's point of view, with philosophical intent—when only fifteen, this sixteen-year-old startled his father by secretly reading Kant. Adjusting the brass screws of the telescope with numb fingers—it teeters up and down like a cannon-barrel aimed at intellectual conquest—stopping for a minute as the night-dark weathercock of the water tower appears in the middle of the cross-lines, he raises the glass eye, sights the Man in the Moon, turns on to the Great Bear, tries to fasten on to the Milky Way—the worker's student son sends out through the extendible brass tubes of the telescope thoughts, emotions, derived from Kant, or from his reading, or thought up for himself—in short, his own home-made universe, never yet drawn on any sky chart (merely flickering across the inside of his own skull, with the speed of light)—sends them out into the shoreless, bottomless darkness of the sky above the water tower. This infinity should come up with answers like morse signals. A dangerous thing to expect, thinks the father, shaking his head. The mother innocently answers his worried 'Where is Franz?' with 'He's sitting on the box balcony in his winter coat and fur cap and mittens, looking at the stars!'

May I revert from the starry universe to the prosaic details of the doctor's apartment? Can I turn straight from the Milky Way to the tin glory of the hip-bath? After the Plough (visibility is measured by focusing on the tiny star above the handle), dare I mention the finger-length nail beside the lavatory (which is inside the flat here, and used only by members of the family and their guests)? Shall I go on? From this nail there hangs a string, and this string is drawn through a bundle of sheets from the *Daily Worker* cut into postcard-size pieces, the prime function of which is no longer to educate the political will—though you can't be sure of that, either. An unambiguous opinion, even trimmed down, is not to be despised, and the review of a performance of *Don Carlos,* cut down into eighths of a page, still pleads as eloquently for freedom of thought as the uncut page.

But, in short, the proportions and way of life are no longer as clear-cut as they were on the *Neue Stern*; the differences of size between firmament and box balcony, water tower and telescope, the son with his philosophical studies and the tin bath, the Milky Way galaxy and post-card-sized pieces of the *Daily Worker* require a mathematical imagination to accommodate them in one equation, to which my knowledge of algebra is not equal.

I should have to find an Impossibility Equation, for the ideal man is an impossible man, never mind whether he is supposed to inhabit the *Neue Stern*, the *Neueste Stern*, or a hole in the ground. It is only the impossible man who will not force a white god on the blacks, only the impossible man who says 'Love your enemies' and does so. The ordinary man sometimes says it too, but he would never behave so impossibly.

Whether the move from the *Neue Stern* to the *Neueste Stern* into the doctor's apartment, acquisition of the companion bookcase, the upright piano, the telescope, relate to the problems of the mean sensual or the ideal man, I dare not decide without some additional and more advanced training in algebra.

Perhaps I should add the lute in the young girl's room to that triumvirate of equivocal objects. Franz, at sixteen, has chosen the telescope for his emblem, the Neighbour's daughter has her lute. Adorned with ribbons, it hangs in place of a picture on the wall of her bedchamber, presenting the light, polished kangaroo belly of its resonance box to the beholder. What are streets for but to walk away from one's parents, out into the wide world. Romantic tableau : Fiddler Tom the Arch-Druid in hiker's disguise silhouetted on the mossy hillock of a neolithic grave, in the middle of a wood, poking the camp-fire with a hazel wand, throws his cap up in the air, a yellowhammer catches it and flies off with it, to fix the Blue Flower to it. . . .

The Century of the Child has become a Century of Youth : books for the young, songs for the young, hiking for the young—'I love to go a-wandering'. 'Modern Youth' reads, draws, paints, sculpts, all in art-nouveau *Jugendstil.* Youth to the fore, particularly in the trenches; but post-war youth advances too. The Neighbour's daughter—who has long fair plaits, wears sandals and embroidered skirts and takes a cold shower in the mornings—is a member of the Junior League of Health and Beauty. So far she has only been kissed by members of her Youth Club, she believes in Youth to the Fore, playing her lute, plucking the strings, Tom Fiddler, ribbons flying in the wind, up hill and down dale. My Makart beauty of a grandmother also owned a lute, but she did not wander up hill and down dale with it —lutes also have marched with the times.

Somewhere between these status symbols of a new family dignity and the immigrant furniture from the *Neue Stern* —with divan cushions and grandfather's bed-bench, Dürer's *Madonna with a Pear,* borders of skating Dutchmen—a whole world of other furniture has proliferated all over the doctor's apartment. Neither fish nor flesh, comparable to crowd extras or office workers—such as I encounter every day in the tram, on the bus, behind ticket or information windows, in wretched government offices, in department stores or clothing shops—and I can only recall those faces, arms and legs by their functions. The tram conductor and his hand clipping my ticket; the flower-woman and the red needle-pierced fingers of her left hand, the black glove on her right hand, cutting the leaves off my roses and breaking off the thorns at the base of the stem; the man in the grey hat and his left foot, which slips on a peanut shell in the grocer's shop, how funny—but I know no more of the man in the grey hat than that his left foot slipped.

In the same way I know very little about the rectangular couch in the daughter's *kabinett*, or the son's brass bed, or the old-fashioned twin beds of the parents, the hall wardrobe with mirror and flowery lining paper, or the lino-covered hall floor. In the other rooms Frau Rabe, the daily, rubs the parquet once a week with floor polish until it shines. I know about these things, but I can get no closer to the essence of couch, brass bed, hall cupboard, hip-bath, dressing-table, umbrella-stand, bedside lamp, solid-fuel stove and hall mirror than to the tram conductor, the flower-woman, the man who slips on the peanut—thus far and no further. I know this is a failing in me—every man is my brother. I should ask the tram conductor, Do you believe in God? Or the flower lady, Is your mother still alive? And the man who slips on the nut, Do you, like me, find our nation's history very instructive? But I am not equal to my task. I leave these people and these ordinary pieces of furniture to their fate.

My interest reawakens when we leave the doctor's apartment on the second floor, waxes as I pass Dr Max Friedenthal's apartment, descending the spiral staircase with its red iron banisters, towards the courtyard, and I must admit that the circle of Schmölzer and the Neighbour at the *Neueste Stern* is now closed—save at one point.

I haven't nosed around the shops yet. They face towards the street, towards the customer. The Co-operative is the hub of all the shops, where all roads, morning walks, gossip, slanders, complaints, tidings of joy, news of love-affairs, case histories of the illnesses of all the fortress ladies, all meet. The shop lies two steps below the level of the asphalt pavement. (And talking of levels, Dr Max Friedenthal does try to play down his bourgeois affiliations, like saying 'Sorry!' when inadvertently jostling someone in a theatre foyer or public conveyance or on the pavement; or asking to be remembered to your mama; or spreading his napkin before the spoon dips into the soup. But the Deputy's wife in any case rather likes all that: napkins, sorrys, remembered mamas.)

In the Co-op store: past the sauerkraut barrel, circumnavigate the glass stand bearing glass jars of fruit drops, stop in front of the live-baby-sized jar of pickled cucumbers, mustard-seed plankton and bayleaf sediment, a wooden gherkin fork like the abandoned anchor of a departed cucumber ship in the brackish cucumber liquor, grey-mould blooming salami sausages, Cracow-Wurst, Extra-wurst, black puddings on black iron hooks (Good morning, *Frau Nationalrat*), boxes of soap-flakes piled in a pyramid, a grease-glistening tin barrel of salad oil. (*Frau Nationalrat* —the Deputy's wife—herself once stood, a salesgirl in a grey overall, sleeves powdered with flour, behind the counter where salami is sliced, blocks of butter cut up, salad oil poured into bottles, and carbohydrates, proteins, vitamins and mineral salts for the fortress garrison distributed, if not actually prepared.)

But the hubbub in the protruding belly of this great

building is really nothing to do with the distribution of food. The Co-op is a communal amenity, thought up, run and extended by comrades for the good of comrades: there is positively no profit motive. The whole national economy could be such a non-profit-making co-operative, but we haven't got that far yet, these inflammatory speeches, war widows' monologues, dialogues of the war disabled, while doing the shopping: the State refuses to raise pensions for disabled ex-servicemen! Have you heard, Frau Kobčiwa, coal is going up! They're sacking people in the locomotive factory! The rich ought to pay for it, just once pay for it all. . . . For six weeks we've had to buy on tick, run up debts—oh, to have everything paid for, by anyone, the State, the Rich, the Party, the Union of Small Shopkeepers, even by the priest, or the Archbishop in his archiepiscopal palace to the left of the unfinished spire of St Stephen's Cathedral—or by the Pope in Rome if need be. To get it all paid off, then one could make a fresh start. You hear it said aloud, repeated, again and again—*Frau Nationalrat*, the comrade with the shopping bag, is standing by and is meant to hear, thus the voices of the people go straight to the ear of the Deputy, and into the Legislative Assembly. Now there is a storm in the cucumber sea, the wooden anchor is hoisted there, the glistening cucumbers are forced singly between the wooden prongs and lifted on to waterproof paper and, sweating cucumber liquor, they are wrapped up. I need a hospital bed for my husband, my husband will intercede for you. The Neighbour, the Deputy, will procure a hospital bed for Frau Kobčiwa's husband, who is a locksmith.

Sailing past the sauerkraut barrel again with black leather shopping-bag full, up the asphalt steps to the pavement, a slightly panting emergence from the washing-powder - sauerkraut - salad - oil - vinegar - and - sausage atmosphere, walk along the fortress wall, past the wire-protected notice-board case of the party group. News for naturalists: Sunday outing to the Lainz Zoo, meet 9 a.m. at Pulverstampf Gate, reduced entrance fee for groups of more than ten people. Important notice: branch meeting every Tuesday at 8 p.m. in the party hall. Political education, officers' reports, full agenda. This notice-board is the whale-mouth of the party, the protective wire-mesh like the filter grating. Only small fry of a digestible size are allowed to pass through, the big fish of the party leadership, philosophical pikes, Marxist sharks, Atheist shads, the economist-eel, stay in the majestic headwaters of the Central Office, they have no business here. In any case, the bag-laden Neighbour's wife casts no glance at this censored notice-mouth. She walks past the branch notice-board, turns left round the corner of the fortress and into the first shop after rounding the corner—the tobacconist's.

This pedlar's tray turned shop sells things that are virtually superfluous, certainly not essential for survival, but one can afford them when one has a job: narcotics, glow-sticks, which, wondrously transformed into blue smoke, billow out from Schmölzer's nostrils, drifting over the leading article of the party newspaper. Virginia cigars in violet boxes, shimmering brown and seductive through the cellophane window of the package.

One thinks of a Virginia with its straw mouthpiece between the thick lips of a two-in-hand cabby complete with bowler and lucky gipsy earring. Crack of the whip. Off we go, Your Honour—a bourgeois vision of servants. Anyhow, the tobacconist—ex-serviceman Podiwinsky with his wooden leg—stocks Virginia cigars, besides a positive army of common brands of cigarette, like *Sport* and *Ägyp-*

tische III, also windproof cigarette lighters, flints, lighter fuel ampoules, stamps—no longer the profile of His Whiskers overprinted 'Deutsch-Oesterreich' (a temporary expedient of the Postmaster-General's Office), but genuine Republican postage stamps. This is Podiwinsky's sole claim to power, that by stamp-proxy he can make letters fly. No longer a monarch's mail service across the one-time Holy Roman Empire of the German people, which began to decline about the same time as the special postal privileges of the Thurn und Taxis ducal family ceased. Friendship, Your Grace, greetings from my wooden leg! The letter flies as before, but no longer over a Holy Roman Empire, or across the multiracial Empire that followed; at best, it crosses the entire Republic from Neusiedler Lake to Lake Constance, and Podiwinsky can take pride in his postal appointment, independent of noble birth.

A Republican letter: in the Republic power belongs to the People, the State belongs to the People, to you and me, the Postal Services belong to the State, it follows therefore that every letter must belong to you and me. Podiwinsky is not conscious of this delegation of power. Otherwise he might take a look at Dr Max Friedenthal's tax returns, or go through the Neighbour's politically important official letters, pass on to the Deputy's wife the contents of love-letters written by the Deputy's daughter, or scrutinise the application made by the charwoman Rabe to the War Widows and Dependents Fund for inaccuracies. But Podiwinsky confines himself to giving out stamps, and is grateful to the Neighbour for getting him the tobacconist's shop —disabled ex-servicemen of good character are given a shop by the State Tobacco Monopoly instead of a pension from the parent State. He is content with the shelter of his kiosk roof, arranges the newspapers on the counter: the

Competitors' Journal, the *Children's Mail*, the *Daily Worker*, the *Daily Sketch*; says to the Neighbour's wife as she comes in laden with shopping bags, Good morning, *Frau Nationalrat*, what can I get for you? A large box of household matches, that's all for today.

Finally next door, the dairy, terminus of the shop round. Clinking empty milk bottles put down, she asks for two litres, the scoop dips into the aluminium milk pail, dispensing, stream of milk directed through a funnel, wait for the white milk to shoot out through the narrow stem. Six rolls to go with it, they crunch as they are pressed against each other, a dozen eggs, white of egg, white of milk, white coat of salesgirl—one could even sell white waistcoats here, where everything is so white.

Intermediate Position and Lesson One

Can politics be practised from gas street lamps?

MOTTO 1

'. . . she said how hopeless life had been among the Whites in Cherson.
They were hanging people in the main roads from the street lamps.
They hanged them, and left them hanging.
When the children came past on their way home from school, they crowded round the lamp-posts and stood there for a long time.
This story is not only true of Cherson, we were told it was no different in Pskov.'

(from *Victor Sklovsky's Sentimental Journey*)

MOTTO 2

'Even what happens at Sirk's Corner is subject to cosmic laws.'

(Karl Kraus)

Can one practise politics from gas street lamps, if one is a boy in a sailor suit? A gas lamp is an object that lights the street, but in a man's political life it can be one of the Last Things, if for instance he is suspended from one. But just as even a practising Catholic of the old school hardly thinks of extreme unction every time he fills his oil lamp (still used in non-electrified provincial homes), so a casual stroller in the multinational Empire, coming from the Sirkecke, hardly thinks at all: *Kiss your hand madame twirling cane raising bowler on my honour as an officer Royal Box rendezvous devotion for the Emperor surpassing love for a married woman I accept your challenge sir exchanging the passwords of the Emperor's Knights of the Waisted Full-Dress Uniform Hello Lieutenant-Colonel old boy tally-ho dear old carrion-comfort death silly anarchist joke jail the brute lovely Désirée rings under her eyes today has she been crying or something?* . . .

Anyway, walking from Sirk's Corner under the plane trees of the Ringstrasse towards the Opera, Parliament, Burgtheater and City Hall, he passes numerous gas lamps, even by daylight, and most certainly when it's getting dark, the gas rises, in 1908 the Municipal Gas Works produced 108,501,000 cubic metres of gas. The total length of arterial pipe in the gas distribution network in 1908 amounted to 608,185 metres. The total number of street lamps in the urban distribution area was 22,398. The gas comes out of the pipes as required, giving a peaceful light, peace-gaslight.

In the *German Medical Weekly* we read:

> The most popular peacetime gases, carbon dioxide, hydrocyanic gas, carbon monoxide, are the least popular in wartime, being much too volatile and easily dispersed. Special significance attached to irritant gas, arsenic trichloride, diphenylchlorarsine and diphenylaminechlorarsine, which has a thoroughly unpleasant but not necessarily dangerous effect on the human being. The sufferer coughs and spits, there is watering of the eyes, running of nose and mouth, and vomiting.
>
> This gas is not sufficiently toxic, and was really only

useful while protective masks could still be permeated by it. Asphyxiating gas, e.g. phosgene, chlorine, bromine, chloropicrin, etc., is partly a true gas and partly finely dispersed particles of liquid, i.e. a vapour, and has a most damaging effect on the respiratory organs, especially the lungs. Its irritant action is subtly calculated so as hardly to affect the sensory organs, so that the victim often does not realise what he is breathing and continues to fill his lungs, unaware. Several hours later the symptoms begin. The lung vesicles become permeable by fluid, and water inexorably enters the lungs from the bloodstream. This combines with the inhaled air to produce a foam, inflating the lung to five or six times its normal size.

The patient (writes Professor Assmann) presents the picture of someone struggling desperately to breathe, with cyanosed lips and cheeks. There is audible rattling in the throat, choking and the extreme restlessness associated with mortal terror. Not without cause. The heart has to overcome both the resistance of the enormously distended lung and the abnormal viscosity of the blood due to loss of fluid. At first it expands, but is finally bound to fail.

Vesicant gas—e.g. dichloroethylsulphide or mustard gas, lewisite, etc.—is never a true gas but always in the form of a vapour. Spread as a spray, wherever its tiny droplets penetrate they cling like a lubricating oil. Here too the effect is not felt for several hours, so that the substance is inadvertently spread further, on to the skin, the face, the mucous membranes, into the eyes. Hands, clothing, objects touched, transfer the droplets to other people, contaminating everything, without anyone being aware of it; and again, after a few hours, the symptoms begin. Wherever a droplet landed, it begins a relentless corrosive action. No power in the world can remove it from the skin. It reddens, blisters, dissolves the skin, the exposed flesh festers and forms infectious abscesses. An agonising decline follows, blindness, internal haemorrhages, pneumonia or septicaemia, to the bitter end.

The gas rises out of the pipes—which proliferate like a fungus mycelium under the Imperial capital—through the ribbed, painted lamp-shaft, flows softly hissing to fill the white porous incandescent mantle and. . . . Let there be light, the nightly rising of the gas moon : swarms of gnats dancing about the lamp bowl, a bowler hat passes below, lower still a cane taps the pavement. The glass bowl might rise to greet the bowler hat—a little more gas would do it, the elevating effects of gas are well known—but in fact the bowler passes unhailed, bowled along by the rhythm of the tapping cane. This gaslit world of the Ringstrasse, if only the pointilliste Seurat could have painted it, sketched it in charcoal, set it down in paint for posterity, or at least in black and white for our descendants! Bowler hat silhouetted against gaslight globe, shadow of a walking-stick, outline of a plane tree—beautiful triumph of the Third Estate. Against a shadow ballet of caryatids on the façades of the splendid new apartment houses, in the Ringstrasse or the Boulevard Haussmann, they plant street lamps like sacred groves : trees of light, sacred to the Third Estate as the oak was to the old Germanic tribes, for now at last night can be transformed to day, gaslight-day, as candles and torches used to do it for the aristocracy of former days. Independent of princely or episcopal candlemakers, torchbearers, lamplighters and those aged church mice who devote their lives to the tending of candles, a municipal gas lamp has to light everybody within range :

swarms of dancing gnats, bowler hats, military shakos, a fez, one-in-hands, two-in-hands, governesses, respectable citizens, policemen, Magyars, Czechs, Bosnians, Italian anarchists, even Orthodox Jews from Odessa, unfortunately even the loving couples who would surely prefer to remain unlit. Simply everybody. So for the bourgeoisie it is not merely pleasurable but a kind of sacred action to stroll along the Ring to the Opera (Temple of Art), Parliament (Temple of Statesmanship), Burgtheater (Art again), City Hall (non-dogmatic Local Politics).

The great political era of gas street lamps is, however, still to come, as the Century of the Child advances. Street lamps shall have a significance reaching far beyond their sphere of light. To tower above the multitude, twice the height of a man, hissing gas, there's a historical task if you like, lighting home defunct lord mayors of Vienna in their glass hearses, Burgtheater actors of Hamlet stature, archdukes and generals, even the venerable bewhiskered Emperor himself, while muffled drums shepherd the prone, earthly husk towards the Capuchine Vaults. Such tasks do not fall to provincial street lamps, of identical design and possessed of similar white, porous, incandescent mantles though they may be.

A gas lamp by the Schlossberg at Graz, for example, what could that possibly illuminate? A retired brigadier, perhaps, sitting on the bench below reading the daily report and forecast of the water level of the Danube and all its tributaries, a Slovenian law student about to take his finals, a primary-school teacher in *lederhosen* and long white socks, reading aloud to his fiancée from an abridged version of the *Edda* and brooding about his fate here on the linguistic frontier. A street lamp in Mährisch-Ostrau probably doesn't even have these chances, and as for the politically underprivileged status of a street lamp in Fiume or Olmütz, the less said the better.

But take a Ringstrasse street lamp, or the lamp at the corner of Herrengasse and Strauchgasse, opposite the Lower Austrian Assembly, where, on an Indian summer day in October, a speaker comes out on the balcony, looks to left and right and shouts: 'As from today we are citizens of a Republic!' A street lamp like that one does not serve merely to light the deaths of emperors and court actors, funeral cortèges and the proclamation of a Republic—sombre but inevitable happenings of this kind can take place equally well in broad daylight—but it does provide something to hold on to. Here in broad daylight, one, two, three men, agile boys, cling to the gloss-painted lamp-post like drowning men to a straw, to look down from above on the Imperial courier, Hamlet's final farewell, the bewhiskered Emperor's last journey. Or look up to a balcony where a man stands shouting, 'As from today we are citizens of a Republic!'

The respectable Sailor Boy is one of those who cling to the lamp-post at the corner of Herrengasse and Strauchgasse on that October day, no longer a boy in a sailor suit, butterfly nets and botanical collections long discarded, he sports an open-necked shirt and Spartan-Spartacist views, though still suffering the baroque emotional excesses of late adolescence. Despite having successfully measured his manhood against the challenge offered by the chambermaid. He has left the venerable Schotten College prematurely, without taking his leaving examination; thus refusing to begin the scheduled advance towards the highest castes, the wielders of power in the multinational Empire—so much for his parents' careful grooming—the very ones who will be done away with this mild October day.

He goes in for near-intellectual jobs like publisher's representative, bookseller, journalist and puppeteer, and at this particular moment his right hand is outreaching the short-fingered groping hand of a man in a military cap—but no cockade, that got torn off, by himself or another—for a free bit of lamp-post. Farther up, just below the light globe, hangs a third man, who keeps slipping, kicking about, feeling for a foothold. His shoes finally find a small groove, he pulls himself up again, slips again, a very Sisyphus of Republican intoxication. The Sailor Boy, equally fervent, is shouting Hurrah! Hurrah! and again, Hurrah for the Republic! Hurrah! as the man above slips and churns about once more.

One might think that even metropolitan gas lamps, property of the City of Vienna, would get tired of political life. Having seen the Republic successfully established, they might retire, hissing soothingly, diffusing a gentle light, letting things take their course. Not so, they perversely begin to demand human sacrifices. They lend their grey-painted shafts as slippery observation posts for every little *putsch* and local quasi-revolution, and as the Century of the Child advances they get steadily worse. They drag in the provincial street lamps, and not only of their own country but of all Europe—excepting only the independent Swiss lamps, the Swedish lamps, and the lamps of that sodden country beyond the Channel—into a gaslit inferno. What a bastard race of street lamps. Not content with looking on and giving light, they demand human sacrifices, like some Mexican idol of green malachite.

And who was the first officer in this century to give the order, String him up on the lamp-post! I dare not reveal, for reasons of security. One never knows where they will draw the age limit for conscription in the next Great

War. . . . But you can see the legion of the hanged, in the showcase of our century, with placards round their necks: I am a Black Marketeer and had to be hanged; I am a traitor and had to be hanged (though we all know that high treason is just a matter of dates); I betrayed my race and had to be hanged (i.e. though of German or racially kindred blood, I slept with a Jewess and had to be hanged); and always of course from a lamp-post. A shorn head lolls forward over the terrorising cardboard label, like a puppet's head when the master's hand is withdrawn. Gas flows softly hissing into the white porous incandescent mantle, and by the light of the gas lamps of Vienna, Graz, Mährisch-Ostrau, Ölmütz, Fiume, Breslau, Warsaw, Kiev and Dniepropetrovsk the puppet head of the hanged man dangles, still dangling the next morning when the gas supply has been turned off, dangles even when all the lamps are dark in broad daylight.

3 The Battle Against Ornament, or, The New Functionalism; also, how one must cast off one's parents in order to live in the Century of the Child (Synthesis)

A sailor-suited boy from a middle-class background, waving his cap, legs crossed monkey-fashion up the lamp-post, shouting 'Long live the Republic!', will eventually have to climb down again to the asphalt pavement, knock his heels together to stir up the pins and needles in his feet, and turn back; Michaeler Platz, Hofburg with Imperial crown in showcase window, the shop, brass shining, red marble, of the Court Confectioner, meringue-light Dobos-torte-smooth, marzipan-gritty, now left behind, he goes through the Herrengasse towards the Ringstrasse, turning right at the Café Central (without entering it), Strauch-gasse lined with banks, passes the Harrach Palace—baroque arrangement of pillars, Harrach in the part of Zeus, Palffy doing Odysseus, Esterhazy some nameless wing-batting genius, Batthiany escorting a Goddess of Fortune with cornucopia, what you might call a full allegorical programme for the medallions of a painted ceiling, all on a deep infinity of blue, the old generations passing—he goes past all that and crosses the street.

He looks up at the yellow sandstone figure of the 'God help me' King, then through the dark archway—ugly, haunting memories of grammar-school days—crosses the Schotten Court, to the Ringstrasse, brief subliminal glimpse of the Votive Church, unsuccessful attempt on the Emperor's life—Amen!—shrimp-strewn entrails of spire, turn east at the Ring—we know the way—towards the Danube Canal, rather a blot on the revolutionary Sailor Boy's escutcheon, that address, sits down in the parental Advocate's apartment, second floor, lunchtime, family time, mealtime, Mama, in front of a gold-rimmed, deep soup-plate and waits for Maria the cook—all cooks are called Maria unless they happen to be called Resi—Maria in this case to start serving the soup with liver dumplings.

('Scrape the skin off a goose liver and chop it finely; cream two ounces of butter or beef dripping until fluffy, add gradually two beaten whole eggs and two yolks; remove the crusts from two rolls, soak them in milk and add to the mixture, with a little chopped green parsley, salt, freshly ground pepper and fine breadcrumbs; stir and mix well. . . .')

Maria, then, dips the wide silver soup ladle mouth into the liver dumpling soup, slowly serving the young master. The liver dumplings, kept back to the last in the ladle-mouth—they must never splash into the soup, throwing up fat globules on to trousers or freshly pressed lapels, Really Maria, says the lady of the house, that must never happen in this house—slowly slide it into the soup.

Has Sailor Boy spent twenty-five years in the Century of the Child, has he left school prematurely, without taking that most sacred final exam; has he, before his former schoolfellows who stayed on in the routine of the hypocritical monks' régime have even entered those clammy old Teutonic woods with Tacitus, measured his manhood not only against the chambermaid but against more desirable arty-crafty students, girls in bookshops and from ballet schools, has he—Long live the Republic!—climbed a lamp-post at the corner of Herrengasse and Strauchgasse: just to sit here in the parental home in front of a gold-rimmed soup-bowl having hot soup with liver dumplings swilled out to him?

A child born in the Century of the Child must be aware of the problems of being a child, otherwise it might as well be a child without a century. A child with parents, simply a child honouring its father and mother, investing this honourable mortgage that your days on earth may be long, as promised by Moses. A boy who honours his father as his prototype, a girl inheriting her mother's virtue, a family round a table, all eyes on the patriarchal beard, in which wisdom seems to gather like moss, to be handled softly, slowly, gently, everyone waiting for the beard to part in a mouthhole, saying *'Mahlzeit!'*, the ultimate wisdom, patriarchal world, Golden Age, schoolbook memories cold as ashes, the Bad Boys Max and Moritz have usurped the pulpit of propriety, called on Struwwelpeter as an ally, ordered Tom Fiddler the Youth Leader to compose a new anthem, and, to the gentle applause of the kind-hearted Maria Montessori, blown Teacher and all his precepts sky-high. Those two fiends have dismissed guardian angels and cherubs to the realms of historical iconography.

We demand our own little Isle of Sodom, our own little Hill of Gomorrah! Max and Moritz roar from the children's pulpit. And the Children's Party, always accompanied by the gentle applause of the kind-hearted Maria Montessori, grows and grows. Instead of school pencils, children make sure they have their little pink sex-rulers, and the paediatricians say 'Good boy'. Instead of honouring father and mother, sons love their mothers passionately, daughters yearn for their fathers. Instead of putting away childish play in order to learn, learning becomes child's play.

Department store owners tremble at the whims of their child customers: Will the sticky new rubber duck find favour? Will the Teddy bear with the two-tone squeak arrive in time? Will the kiddie sword sell adequately?

Dress designers lose sleep thinking up new fashions for children, and they will not rest until even ageing *cocottes* trip along the pavement in children's dresses, pit-a-pat. University lecturers do not conceal their childishly cropped hair behind the black side-pieces of their hornrims—round-headed and beardless they strive to resemble their children. The Children's Party is bound to be victorious in the Century of the Child. It's a long time since children were doomed to be miniature adults, a long farewell to children's frock coats and top hats; nowadays the adults are determined to become children, to evade that fundamental challenge of the century: Murder—which has become unmanageable single-handed—Murder, be it by poison gas, atom bomb or radiation.

How can Sailor Boy escape from the family table, where the Century of the Child has not even begun? How can he escape the soup with liver dumplings, ready served out? Where is the exit from the patriarchal labyrinth? Perhaps he should take a room of his own, he could afford it on his salary, but all the comfortable perks—bathroom, drawing-room, Maria the cook—would go by the board. Perhaps refuse to have his meals at the family table and retire to the nursery to guzzle cold sliced sausage off greaseproof paper? Not a good solution, the cold meat variations, Cracow-Wurst, Extrawurst, ham and salami, are not sufficiently tempting. Perhaps start his own family altogether. How does one manage that in the Century of the Child? Child marriages are no problem, but child parents are: who rules whom, who has to be sick first when Max and Moritz eat too many chicken legs—the Bad Boys themselves, or the parents constitutionally unable to say no?

Such problems cannot be solved by theorising, or by discussions between fathers and children, or by consulting an encyclopedia, under Father, Child, Parenthood, Sovereignty, Intrigue, Apportionment, Entail, Parental Rights, Age of Majority—and what about the Age of Minority?—Compulsory Education, Duty to Support One's Children—shouldn't there be a duty to entertain them as well? Couldn't Max and Moritz have a right to demand some clowning from Father when life in a cot becomes too unbearably tedious? Theory butters no parsnips, one still sits at the parental table, decanting the liver dumplings out of the fat-scummed soup, longing to get rid of one's parents. The determination to be free from parents is not confined to middle-class boys in sailor suits: bear cubs, leverets, children of building labourers, salesmen and tram conductors, even Royal children, the young of moles, anteaters, judges, doctors, tightrope walkers, even children's children—when the time is ripe, all children suddenly want to be rid of their parents, for good.

The grammar-school girl from the *Neueste Stern,* too, wearing plaits and sandals, still a member of the Junior League of Health and Beauty, has similar ambitions: to be off with the Youth Group, the *Students' Song Book* in her rucksack, lute ribbons flying in the breeze, flat-heeled walking shoes, dirndl skirt and light socks, pea soup with ham sausage in a mess-tin. On an improvised stone hearth bluish flames are rising from the damp firewood, the pea soup beginning to bubble, the bubbles also rising from the marsh in the ghostly night; one can observe pantheistic feelings coming to the boil simultaneously with the pea soup. Here one has come a long way from one's parents.

The socialist senior schoolchildren and students have rented a mountain hut owned by the Ramblers' Fellowship in the alpine foothills, for the weekend. There is still snow on the rounded peak of Oetscher, alpine jackdaws freewheel upwards with the wind, up rock faces yellow with alpine primulas.

The group leader Max turns the key of the hut in the lock; open the wooden shutters, fetch water, start a fire, unpack the food, someone has brought field-glasses, adjust the screw, everyone in turn can have a look, up at the snow-covered peak of Oetscher. The alpine jackdaws see-saw in the polished bull's eye of the Zeiss binoculars. The group leader says to the Neighbour's daughter: I'll hold the binoculars for you, just turn that black screw until it's in sharp focus; this is how he offers his love. Felix the philosophy student takes a spade to the back of the house in the afternoon and with some difficulty buries himself up to the neck in black woodland soil and fir needles, calls his friends and discourses—a head only, peering like a mushroom from the ground—on the extinction of the body, Indian asceticism, yoga and *hara-kiri*, Lao-tse and Tao, Gandhi and his magnificent fight against the white man, against us; and that is *his* way of saying I love you. Everyone listens attentively. Neither Max the group leader nor the other members of the weekend expedition query Felix the philosophy student's self-burial, everyone is free to seek and follow his own way, the essence of individuality may be hidden in the forest soil, under the snowy summit of Oetscher, under the wings of the alpine jackdaws, in the stamens of the alpine primulas: Seek and ye shall find. Happy Felix.

It isn't absolutely essential to stick to the Party Line at these weekends. In the evening by the dying wood-fire the drama student Otto recites passages from Rilke's *Cornet*; the Neighbour's blonde daughter is leaning against a tree, her blue eyes glancing across Otto and the dying campfire, not that one can see any blue in this darkness, but everyone knows that her eyes are blue. Otto's wooing is certainly more direct, less ambiguous, than Max's or Felix's. After all, he has been trained, he doesn't go such a tortuous way about things, nor does he wear glasses that have to be removed before he can kiss anybody. Troubadour games among the socialist students, Max, Felix and Otto at the Tournament, the Court of Love in the Ramblers' hut, here is another way to get away from one's parents, at least for the weekend.

But on Sunday evening, Monday morning at the latest, one has to return to the parental home, up the stairs to the second floor, back into the doctor's apartment, back to the *Neueste Stern*. There is no more joy in mounting these stairs than those of the Ringstrasse. The filial stair progress leads to the compulsion of the family table, whether the liver dumpling is eased into the soup by Maria the cook or one's own mother, the child's imprisonment is the same. There have been heroic prisoners, of course, Richard Cœur de Lion at Dürnstein, Martin Luther in the Wartburg, Napoleon on Elba; muscatel and jugged hare, or even snipe. Larded pheasant and Moselle wine, served by a jailer with a clanking bunch of keys, may taste better than herrings and water, but Florestan's aria on Liberty—which I suspect he will have to repeat, even after his release—is what both the Sailor Boy and the high-school girl would burst into, were they required to sing at table.

In short, so long as the Century of the Child is not built on a legal foundation, the freedom of youth remains a toy elephant with feet of clay; so long as parents aren't taxed on not being contradicted by their children, the State does not pay pensions direct to those suffering from being under twenty-one, going to school is not rewarded by prizes and mothers below the age of fifteen are suspended from further grammar-school studies, the Century of the Child will remain a mockery, and all the idealistic efforts of heroic children to get rid of their parents will sink without trace.

What is left for a Sailor Boy, even one who has come of age, but to go to the quayside of the Danube Steamship Navigation Company and say to the captain of a pleasure steamer or barge: I have had enough of my parents, I want to go to sea. A sandal-shod grammar-school girl has not even this possibility of daydream escape; no chance of dancing classes at fifteen, left-hand waltzing, kissing of kid-gloved hands, to take a turn round the room between dances, flirt at a house party ball, may I see you home after the dancing class, all that is already past. Dancing-class flirtation, call it a cunning arabesque of courtship among the bourgeoisie and minor aristocracy, curbed lust, putting a neatly trimmed formal hedge around growing desire: a happy ending for the sixteen-year-old countess, married at seventeen, and exactly nine months later the chubby son and heir lies on the pillow marked with a coronet. But who thinks of such Church-sanctioned ways out round a camp-fire in the alpine foothills, who would permit such trashy schoolgirl thoughts when one is studying Büchner's *Woyzek* for the German finals, analysing it with passion, positively adoring it?

Can there be a compromise? Is the desire to go dancing, go to a ball, wear make-up, not a stronger world of Will and Idea than the world of literary revolutionaries of the *Hessische Landbote*? How long can a pretty blue-eyed blonde put up with students who take off their glasses to kiss, wear open-necked shirts and can't dance, read aloud from *The Cornet*, do the schoolgirl's maths homework for her and venture no further, whether for fear of the insecurity of an intellectual career, or through precocious insight into the enigma of sacred and profane love. One hopes to solve that after taking finals.

A middle-class Sailor Boy can do better than that, he can take off his sailor suit and there is a dinner-jacket ready for him, perhaps even tails—anyhow, a new dress-persona to lean on.

Even this lamp-post-scaling rebel—Long live the Republic!—could take advantage of these conventions. But he prefers to dress up, he goes into the office of a theatrical costumier and says, 'I'd like a Scottish costume for tonight's Arts Ball', wraps the red tartan kilt about his body, ties on the sporran, puts on bulging, thick woollen knee-length socks, sets a round cap on his head, throws the bagpipes over his shoulder, mugs up a few well-tried Scottish jokes and some relevant facts about the Loch Ness monster, then at the cash desk of the College of Art—no carnival without its Arts Ball, artists have been designing the decorations for weeks, three nights, three separate themes, Round Dance of the Nations, Savage Races, Seafarers and Landlubbers, one can see how the idea of the League of Nations can influence an Arts Ball—at the cash desk, then, he takes a single man's ticket, which, as usual, is 10 per cent cheaper than a lady's ticket, not to mention the cheapness of a student's ticket.

But what do I see, the blonde blue-eyed schoolgirl coming to this ball? Has she betrayed the Youth Movement? Who brought her here? A law student disguised as an Argentinian gaucho, a Hungarian shepherd who reads Mathematics in everyday life, perhaps even one of those elderly clowns with a red light bulb built into the tuberous nose which lights up, winks, gives morse signals about certain free and unescorted Arab girls.

But who the hell would bring a member of the Junior League of Health and Beauty to the Arts Ball? The settings on this particular night are distant lands of papier mâché, Haitian isles of plywood, igloos of hessian, Chinatown made out of reeds from the Neusiedler Lake, an unemployed waiter, made up for tonight as Calafatti the Chinese giant of the Prater merry-go-round, long Chinaman's pigtail but no slit eyes, serves sweet-and-sour pork with bamboo shoots.

The Danube countries are crowded into one single room, the river itself, defying gravity, meanders as an illumination across the plaster ceiling. A gipsy band from Mörbisch-am-See makes Czardas princes of all men, to order, hand behind the ear, three steps to the right, three steps to the left, wild gipsy cries, *Prost!*—feudalism and gipsy frivolity, some evening and night diversion for socialist students, I must say!

Otto the drama student, the only one who can dance—and no wonder, he has to be able to dance, and to fence, too, and to say, Kiss your hand, Madame, in an aristocratic tone, that's all in the day's work for a possible future juvenile lead at the Troppau Civic Theatre—anyhow it was Otto who brought his friends along: 'At a fancy dress ball it doesn't matter whether you can actually dance!'

Thus he tempted the whole group. Felix the philosophy student walks from room to room as an itinerant toy vendor from the colourful Croatian backwater of Zips, with a pedlar's tray—his complex costume copied from an 1815 colour engraving of street-cries. Still rather inhibited, he crosses the hall of Danube countries, behind him Max the group leader as Robinson Crusoe, then the Neighbour's daughter as a blonde Greek maiden, her bare arms covered with brown make-up, a gold fillet in her hair, white ankle-length draped gown like the Attic maidens in the Parthenon frieze.

Neither Felix the toy vendor nor Max-Robinson-Crusoe has asked the blonde Greek girl to dance: they have no dancing class experience behind them, and dread an entanglement of extremities. Otto, as a Corsican pirate, has long since disappeared in dark side-chambers, island worlds, dreamlands.

The music grows noisier, here and there a clown begins to sway, in the turmoil of dancers lamplit noses shine like beacons, Arab girls strewn with confetti sit giggling on the marble steps of the main staircase. Then Max has the inspiration—always the conscientious group leader—of looking for old friends, former schoolmates, acquaintances, desperately seeking a dancing partner for the Greek maiden, and he discovers the Scotsman in the Hall of Danube Lands, with his hand behind his ear, dancing the Czardas, and he introduces the Scot to the Greek. Max recognised his school friend under the Scottish disguise and thought, perhaps the Scot can make my Greek girl a dancer tonight, it's more than I can.

As the Scotsman and the Greek maiden drift via Hungary, Romania and Bulgaria, briefly touching Yugoslavia too, to vanish in the Black Sea next door, to dance, hop about and around, Max sits down on the edge of the platform—where the gipsy music fiddles away—lights a cigarette, gazing into the half-darkness, watching the dancing, swirling *mélange* of nations, blowing smoke-rings through his nose, vaguely sad even before the hangover.

Scotland and Greece—misty moors and the Blue Aegean, moorhens, partridges and the bird of Zeus, whisky and nectar, frugal citizens with pink complexions and nut-brown idlers, the Loch Ness monster and the Sirens—what contrasts. . . . The bourgeois Sailor Boy in Scots clothing will not let the Neighbour's daughter go, he dances through the night, through the entire Arts Ball, with her alone, going on to become her real-life suitor in the ensuing weeks and months, and then to marry her.

So they have achieved, more or less in one night, almost by accident, in a sort of intoxication, casually, as though unplanned, what hitherto they have striven for in vain, whether by climbing lamp-posts—Long live the Republic! —or by Youth Movement weekends: they have virtually succeeded in freeing themselves from their parents.

However, the parents, the bourgeois Advocate on his office-Omphalos and his lute-playing consort on the one hand, and the teetotal Deputy from the working-class district on the other, as also his still more aspiring wife, *Frau Nationalrat*, when they hear this news, when the *fait* is *accompli*, after the marriage, they are not altogether delighted.

But it is easier to take up a strong position as a couple, shooting poisoned arrows from the younger generation fortress, free oneself from one's parents despite all protest, and join battle hand in hand. The battle is joined in the drawing-room of the Schottenring apartment.

Among the marble cake, whipped cream and good coffee, while the lute-playing mother, now mother-in-law as well, urges on to more marble cake, darkly marbled Sunday-best cake, the new apartment is under discussion.

'Well, darlings,' says the Makart beauty of a mother, 'the question of a home is easily solved, we'll simply partition off a part of the office for you, and you can have some of my furniture!'

The Neighbour's daughter, from now on referred to as Sailor Boy's wife, is a young married woman now—when, by the way, will Sailor Boy officially cease to be a boy?—drinks half a cup of coffee with cream after this revelation, a morsel of marble cake must have gone down the wrong way, she has to cough, cough in protest, one doesn't get rid of parents and then set up house with one's parents' furniture, striped-rep period sofas, what next, jingling tea-trolleys with silver-plated handles perhaps, some old chandelier, bourgeois light-fitting-cum-glockenspiel, the glass rhomboids jostling one another whenever door or window is open, cherrywood beds with carved foot-knobs and oval removable bedheads, to hell with all that!

A young generation conscious of its youth does not live among family possessions, those feudal customs are played out: the christening robe descending from generation to generation, yellow and torn inheritance, walking-stick with ivory knob engraved with the arms of the baron (afterwards count), all that always descends to the heir, as also the shrine in the house chapel and the chapel with it, and the estate, the land, the cattle, the wood, perhaps even shares in the Danube Steamship Navigation Company, worthless paper nowadays, we don't want that anyway, we refuse to have it. Today's apartment is not like yesterday's: every bowl, every plate, every salt-cellar, every shoe-scraper, every bathtub and consequently the soul, heart, conscience and the senses of the bather, must be functional in shape and true to the material used, as the architect Bruno Frischherz puts it, and that is the way we want it.

They argue for some time, architects' fees at a time of national economic crisis, pretentious nonsense, eyewash, humbug, think the two fathers, and take no further interest; but Sailor Boy's wife succeeds in imposing Bruno Frischherz. The Youth Movement is a united fighting front, Bruno Frischherz is a member of it and is given the go-ahead to celebrate his aesthetic mass in those two rooms with two *kabinetts* and a lobby. The second floor of a Ringstrasse house becomes a temple of the aesthetic cult. Behind a façade of asphalt-bosomed caryatids, scrambled-egg frieze and acanthus fillets, behind neo-baroque entrance pillars, Bruno Frischherz can open hostilities against ornament.

Ornament is a crime. The hypocritical old morality, bourgeois wife, virgin to the altar or the synagogue, and at the same time the pleasures of the brothel, celebrating promotion at Madame Rosa's establishment, dress-sword around naked belly, that sort of thing could only survive behind dusty Makart bouquets, among swelling, upholstered couches and Tabriz rugs, in front of glass cabinets with laughing fake Chinamen. Bruno Frischherz is against all that. Modern Art for Modern Man, women and girls without corsets, houses, apartments and furniture free from non-functional elements, ladies riding astride like men, chairs simple, straight and spine-fitting, that is the style of this circle, uncorseted girls on bicycles, the unornamented right-angled edge of cupboards displayed with pride, hinges not disguised but flaunted, the brass highly polished.

These symbols of a new world, says Bruno Frischherz, are just as significant as the idea of a League of Nations, or Gandhi's policy of non-violence. Bare brick, he says, used with full respect for the material, means as much to me as confession does to a practising Catholic.

Can Sailor Boy's wife, or indeed Sailor Boy himself—though architecture is not the mainspring of his existence—resist such arguments, the chance to purge the sins of the world with undecorated walls, to achieve everlasting spiritual harmony by rocking to and fro in a strictly functional rocking-chair, to quench eternal thirst by pouring from a plain earthenware teapot? Who, in view of such prospects, could possibly want period sofas, inlaid baroque chests, glass cabinets and cut-glass chandeliers, even as a gift?

Bruno Frischherz is commissioned to redecorate the new apartment according to his modern ideas, as high priest of the New Functionalism. The Sailor Boy's wife thinks, what a pity, those caryatids on the outside, all that ghastly façade-ornamentation, those old pillars will have to stay, what a shame, Bruno, that you can't scrape off the lot to reveal the bare brick underneath.

For months Bruno celebrates his Black Mass, and then: I have done up a new apartment, says Bruno Frischherz, who'll come to a whisky and foxtrot party, come all ye faithful, come!

Sedately thumping, steel-cable creaking, on a March evening before spring has begun, the lift which is still working (lifts in Ringstrasse mansions seem to live for ever, machines fitted with immortal souls, very different from cars born on conveyor belts, like so many hooting, ephemeral flies)—this Methuselah among lifts jerks upwards like a gouty Imperial councillor, wheezing from ground floor to mezzanine, from floor to floor, sometimes getting stuck between floors, cries for help from the lift diving-bell, the caretaker slouches sullenly up to the loft, to heave the monster up to the next floor by means of the oily handwinch, and the senile lift, its heart-attack over, continues. The feeble light bulb may flicker, the mirror in the lift is scratched and blind at the corners, the red plushy upholstery of the semicircular corner seat threadbare, but there's life in the lift mechanism yet. A sulky existence, not really very different from that of an inlaid baroque cupboard, a gilt-edged tabernacle, an old gilt globe, or indeed any of the goods and chattels of the Imperial Councillor's or Imperial and High Court Advocate's apartments to left and right—a piece of machinery that has developed the soul of an Imperial Councillor. Oh, if the Luddites knew of this strange birth, this metamorphosis in reverse, this conservative revolution : to continue a lift-lifetime of service like a ninety-year-old sacristan, immortal according to the teachings of the Holy Catholic Church. Thus, one March evening this lift hauls up a phalanx of young people, among them Felix the philosophy student, Otto the drama student, and even Max, the quasi-cuckold, and various girls with bobbed hair, very necessary for the foxtrot; the lift hauls them all up to Bruno Frischherz's whisky-and-foxtrot party, or Sailor Boy's party, or Sailor Boy's wife's party, take your pick.

The class structure, the Spanish Court ceremonial, is quite meaningless here, amid modern life with modern furniture, interior decoration free from ornament, new wine in old bottles—all that calls for celebration. White, glossy lacquer white, is the colour of the day, a white rack with brass knobs in the entrance hall, hessian background, the battered hats of revolutionary young men hang there, also the arty-crafty daring head-cups, head-pots, head-bowls of the bob-haired girls; a white-painted tub in the corner receives umbrellas, an upturned wooden pyramid, painted white and with the apex cut off (a pyramid can't balance on it's apex), surrounds a pot containing an azalea plant.

Frischherz is standing beside the Sailor Boy's wife in the doorway between hall and living-room : pepper-and-salt suit of English cut, the orange woollen tie is redolent of the South, he stands there looking tanned. His Master's

Voice gramophone horn blares out foxtrot music, my legs your legs my legs your legs, one, two, three, four, hop hop, trot hop, one, two, three, four, in the white room, which has no ceiling light. Illumination issues from the corners, from joins in the furniture, perhaps even from the gramophone loudspeaker, from the faces of the girls, the keyholes, all the lighting is indirect, even divining-rods could not discover its sources.

To conceal the sources of light is not only Bruno Frischherz's master stroke of interior decoration, it far transcends the craftsman-limited horizon of the usual architect's games. The centre of the room is an odious place, that's where the jingling chandelier, tinkling with every draught, dangles in the drawing-room of the adjacent parental apartment, the middle of the room is always a fateful spot, take the Emperor's State Dining-Room in the Hofburg, the Gold Chamber at Schönbrunn, the ballroom of the Campaign Riders' Club at the Palais Pallavicini, there's always a chandelier hanging dead centre, a chandelier-general, representing the Old Order, a bewildering hypnotic element in the iridescent rainbow colours of its cut-glass pendants, always at the exact centre of the room. By this means Court balls, or Republican diplomatic receptions, aristocratic wedding soirées at the Palais Pallavicini, or if necessary, rulers' abdications too (they still reek of the Old Order, though maybe the wrong end of it), can be illuminated.

But for Bruno Frischherz the centre of the room is beyond the pale. Doing away with the centre, he instructs the Sailor Boy, is the first step towards a new individualism; my interior decoration is a centreless creed, an inside without a centre within a completely geometric exterior, a cube, or even better, a sphere or an ovoid. My kingdom for a man who commissions me to build him a villa in the shape of an egg! For the present, Bruno Frischherz has to be content with a Russian egg, peeled glossy white, lying on a plate amidst mounds of yellow mayonnaise, and he falls upon this Russian egg with such gusto that no one could think it less important to him than that hypothetical egg, the ideal shape for a house, of which he was speaking so forcefully.

The bobby-girls slide the left leg backwards, third step in the foxtrot. Otto the drama student is having a whale of a time, putting on another record as soon as the last one dies away inside the horn, my legs your legs, my legs your legs. Felix, the ascetic philosopher, doesn't want to be a spoilsport, drinks whisky for the first time in his life, it doesn't taste of much. He recalls the utterance of his sophisticated schoolfellow, Baron Giovanni Koschier, already a well-known racing driver, who was given a trip to Paris for passing his final school exams. There he visited the fabulous, mirror-resplendent, palm-warmed establishment 'Sphinx', where among other things he had some whisky, and when his former schoolmates, still good little grammar-school boys, ask him What does it taste like? he replies : Like pins and needles in your feet.

Bruno watches the bobbed heads, dashing fringe on forehead, in the corners of the room, quickstep, changing direction. Otto the drama student steers Sailor Boy's wife round a corner, while Sailor Boy himself stands in the glossy white lacquered doorway, also watching. Does he really like Frischherz's universe of starkly plain furniture, these knee-high white-painted storage chests without handles (perhaps one should call them knees rather than chests?), oblong storage units for coarse-weave linen cloths, napkin rings of natural wood, simple cutlery with angular handles, and on top of them thick glasses and flat earthenware bowls for fruit or short-stemmed flowers? Does he like that right-angled couch over there, like a battlement torn out of context, but made of wood, white lacquer glossy, with three wide seat cushions of white leather, even the tea-trolley is of white wood? And in the corner—really, Sailor Boy has to smile at Bruno Frischherz's insensate mania for white—in the corner, resting on a crude red brick of all things, a true find among the props of the multiracial Empire, unexpected and weird, is the white biscuit bust of the young Emperor Franz Joseph, imported from the Advocate's drawing-room next door.

Over there the biscuit bust was at any rate still a significant souvenir, to be respected: Here am I, your Emperor, youthful, handsome, by the Grace of God—Go then, my faithful servant, Mosaic doctor of laws, make an honest living and keep faith with me.

But here, on top of a raw red brick bearing the imprint of the Commune of Vienna, at the corner of a knee-high lacquer rampart, is that a worthy pedestal for the last great (though now dead as a doornail) monarch of the multiracial Empire, with Görz and Gradiska and Krain, Bohemia and Hungary, Lodomeria, Pressburg and Ausschwitz among his litany of titles? Even Bruno Frischherz finds some emotional difficulty in assimilating this final touch of interior decorator's ingenuity. He sees the Sailor Boy's glance alight on the white bust and, feigning drunkenness, he staggers over to the gramophone, rips the arm—screech of needle—off the record, and turns on the dismayed flappers, shouting: 'Friends, the climax of the evening will be a coronation! Who amongst you has noticed the presence of Franz Joseph I in all his youthful beauty in this ornament-free living-room? Look around!

Look in the corners! Isn't that him, over there, done in white biscuit? I brought him across from the Makart Salon, if you'll pardon the expression'—turning to the Sailor Boy—'in order to divest him of his "Franz-Josephness". Forget it's a portrait, ignore the features. Just look at the white of that biscuit porcelain, white in a white room, white within white, manifesting itself as a white stain!'

He goes even closer to the bust, takes something green out of his coat pocket, dumps it on the head of the bust, and shouts, acting even more drunk: 'In the name of the Republic—Long live the Republic!'

'Long live the Republic!' echoes Sailor Boy.

Frischherz continues: 'I crown thee with a laurel wreath of felt. A laurel wreath is an ornament—ornament is a crime. With this criminal, Republican coronation I therefore put this monarch's head beyond the pale! I declare this biscuit bust with felt laurel wreath to be "Abstract Composition No. 1 in White and Green", and herewith divest it of any and every symbolical significance!'

The bobby-girls applaud, Sailor Boy's wife cries 'Bravo' and 'Long live the Republic', Sailor Boy admires the ingenious sophistry of the intellectual Bruno, who now puts the needle back on the record in a new groove, the gramophone burbles forth again, and the girls are glad that Bruno's speech is over.

Do you think Felix is cleverer than Bruno? Granted he goes on a bit when he's had a few drinks, but Bruno towers above us all. . . . Nevertheless, they are only too pleased that the foxtrot now resumes, instead of Bruno's speech about the white stain.

Opposite the memorial corner is the dining-table, an act of artistic self-denial on the part of Frischherz, a gesture towards the master of the household, who cannot bear white tables, they ruin his appetite. Hospital tables, yes, nursery tables, yes, but *not* a white dining-table, it wouldn't go with brown Schnitzel, black Sachertorte, yellow Gumpoldskirchner wine; a brown wooden table, therefore, with beautifully polished grain. But the lamp above it shows architect's freedom regained, two concentric brass rings, covered with white silk, a brass rod down the middle and a brightly polished red wooden knob at the bottom, like a rose-hip—a handle for sliding the brass-trimmed white silk shade up and down.

Raise the lamp by means of the red rose-hip knob, and the light falls on a watercolour. An obscene drawing, the Advocate father will remark on his first visit; You really like that? the Neighbour's wife will say on her first visit. A shamelessly recumbent female, hands clasped under her head, red skirts drawn up to expose the *mons veneris* with luxuriant bush of pubic hair, a half-naked man facing the other way, with a reddish-brown blanket draped over shoulder and hip, eyes penetrating as wasp stings, the title pencilled in block letters underneath: VALLY AND HERMIT. Bruno brought along this watercolour and hung it, complete with lengthy explanations: Vally the model, the Hermit a self-portrait of the artist Egon Schiele, who died at such a tragically early age.

This is modern art—a marvellous, slashing line, daring use of colour on top of an allegedly daring subject. For these crimes the petty bourgeois, mealy-mouthed, holy liars crawling out of Neulengbach village church incarcerated the artist for two weeks in the local jail. But a new age needs a new style of art. Not that Sailor Boy and his wife are all that certain about it, they too find Vally and the Hermit just a trifle dubious, but in order to break away from one's parents one really must kick over the traces at some point.

But where is the focal point of this no-nonsense living-room—can there be a focal point in a room without a centre? Where is the origin of all these co-ordinate points, once Bruno Frischherz, certainly an intellectual nerve-centre himself, though he rejects the idea of centrepoints, has left—for once equally sated with whisky and talking—and the shadows of the bobby-girls are no longer dancing up and down the snow-whitewashed walls?

Is there nothing here that corresponds to the Neighbour's book-altar, nothing like the glass cabinet in the drawing-room of the Advocate's apartment, with fat-bellied China-men and china shepherdesses—some word or some similar container, of little practical use yet that much deeper in significance? Here again I don't have to feel embarrassed, I can take the chalk-covered pointer from the Natural History cabinet at the Schotten College without hesitation and aim it like a musket from the Historical Museum of the City of Vienna in the mock-Gothic Town Hall, and ask meaningly: Over there, beside the white-tiled fireplace, there are some open bookshelves—what about those, then?

A book should be a part of life, says Frischherz, so he hangs bookshelves on invisible screws on the walls of his centreless rooms. Sailor Boy has put his collection of first editions of German poets on these shelves: Hölty, Klop-stock, Platen, Mörike, even forgotten ones like Tümmel in first edition, with uncut, sometimes foxed, paper, uneven digits in the date on the title-page, frequently an old oval-framed owner's stamp; Körner's *Mit Leier und Schwert* is the latest acquisition. These delights leave the book-altar with the gilt-edged classics in red bindings or the glass cabinet with the fat, laughing, fake Chinamen so far behind on the lower slopes of the intellectual mountain that it would need opera-glasses to identify them, far far below.

Take up the volume of Goethe's love lyrics and, deriving fresh strength and inspiration, leave the bobby-girls' Walpurgis Night—ah, if only it were!—and continue rooting around in this apartment.

The ankle-level of the beds must have some significance, too, perhaps to make an accessible playground for children, safe from any danger of falling off; or, if you transfer your love-life to just above floor level, hygienic, Japanese-style, does it make it child's play? Or is it that parents and children are meant to live together in true friendship on a common level? Bending your knees to get into the low-slung, tubular-steel bed may be a cult action.

In the high beds of the parents (Advocate) or the parents (Neighbour) a skilled genealogist could trace forbears like Louis XIV's four-poster at Versailles, and that of the beautiful, motherly Maria Theresa at the Hofburg, *Amalientrakt*, a place of rest, creaking and snoring in authoritarian style even after the removal of the canopy and the heavily fringed curtains, even though the courtly wedding rites may be dropped, the entire Court having to watch the defloration, the high pedestal sleeping-place as a monument to virginity. The parents, resembling Etruscan sarcophagi, can sit up in their night-gowns, appearing even grander and more sublime than by day, raise their index fingers and say, Be good, and then fall back on to downy pillows, no longer visible to the worm's eye view of the children, like gods, who also say Be good, demanding with nocturnal menaces like Hamlet's father, but then sinking back into their featherbed heaven, snoring, but without any loss of dignity or authority.

But no, in the Century of the Child a chubby-cheeked,

demanding two-year-old has to be able to look down on its father's bed. If the father does sit up, pretty wretched specimen of Etruscan graven image, and tries to raise his finger to say 'Be good', the two-year-old, chubby and demanding, taps him smartly on the mouth and says, 'Same to you!'

During the day the beds are covered with an orange silk spread having its own white open-work ornamental cover. Bruno wanted an earth-coloured, firm linen fabric, but this bedspread, a wedding present from an aunt, demanded house-room, and it's easier to love an aunt than one's parents. An orange bedspread as a mother's present would have been turned down for sure, as an aunt's present illustrates the butterfly-wing shimmering fragility of all things in the whirlpool of daughter-and-niece feelings. However, decorative cushions or frilly dolls on the orange bedspread are not permitted.

Apart from this there are no compromises. Looking around from the bed-square one sees no cupboards, no bedside tables with lamps: Frischherz caused all those bourgeois linen and loose cover and featherbed cover and shirt and underwear and sock containers, those unspeakably wicked, shrill, falsetto-squeaking cupboards to sink and vanish into the walls, never to return.

A dressing-table with movable side-mirrors, standing at a slant beside the window to get maximum light, is the only piece of furniture in the room beside the beds. A stool upholstered in dark blue goes with it. I must admit, although I had my doubts, that the beds have ultimately retained their position as navel of the apartment world, low though they may be. Frischherz kicked everything that looked like a cupboard into the wall, like some obtrusive cur, and thus preserved the dominant role of the beds.

The form of the bed seems to resist permanent revolution—a real snag for left-wing circles. True, one can raise or lower the bed—it is low in this case—but there are natural limits to length or shortness and even to width, and in the case of a double bed the best position would be in the middle of the room. Alas for Frischherz and his creed of the missing centre! Perhaps a corner or recess would be best, then; a certain charm, but only for a time, for young couples—what fun to climb over each other. The modern philosophy of functional form also bounces off the bed: a hammock, a camp-bed, a bunk, a sleeping-bag, heap of straw or haystack, each fulfils the function, and each shape is quite adequate to give me a good night. Even the Bed of Procrustes, which has never yet been mass-produced, fits into this demonstration, showing that the architect's dreams of infinite variability—all shapes of house from the cube to the egg—are called to heel by the Bed. For the mythological personification of the Bed I imagine an old country doctor with homoepathic leanings, who growls at me: Sleep or forever hold your peace!

Beyond the bathroom barrier—a Frischherz bathroom, white tiled, how could it be otherwise, is not merely washroom, shower-room, toothbrushing cave: young couples born in the twentieth century elevate the bathroom to a cult, like sunbathing. The Advocate father and the Neighbour have a bath perhaps twice a week, the Sailor Boy and his wife bath every day, full of cult ideas like opening the pores in the skin, relaxing tense nerves, stirring up warm and cold centres on the skin surface, then the fresh linen can stimulate the well-towelled body. Sun worship, physical culture, daily matins in the bathroom: a bathroom in a Ringstrasse house becomes a water chapel, without consecration by either bishop or rabbi. Anyhow, beyond the bathroom barrier, beyond the water chapel, there is still the world of servants. What can one expect there—servants' postcards as in the apartment on the other side of the lift-shaft, a Virgin from Maria Zell, a glass rosary, His Holy Apostolic Majesty in coppergravure? A man like Bruno Frischherz would never stand for that, such freedom of bad taste would leave no room for him.

My ideal patron, says Frischherz, is a man who lets me design everything for him, from his writing-paper and his shoehorn to his town villa, his country house, even the body-work of his car. I believe in a dictatorship of taste; an age like ours—where the furnishing store of Wertheimer in Berlin will modernise one man's ancient castle, and anti-quate another's apartment on the Kurfürstendamm, with chameleon multiplicity—deserves no better.

The maid's *kabinett*, like the water chapel, the low-slung beds, the white living-room, bears the aesthetic brandmark 'Frischherz', though somewhat diminished: a divan bed, a gloss-lacquered cupboard, a specimen of the then still un-known 'Frischherz chair' with functional hollows for back and bottom in a strictly right-angled frame, buttercup-yellow curtains of coarse weave, reading lamp set in the wall, even a bookcase, though only with two shelves. The bourgeois Sailor Boy would like to economise on the furnish-ing of the maid's room. That's just what I won't have, says his wife, remembering Büchner's *Woyzek*, Schmölzer's poverty, the move from the *Neue* to the *Neueste Stern*, even the principles of the Junior League of Health and Beauty come into it—you have a duty not only towards the community but towards your own body, the basis of idealistic thinking.

In the end it will cost us just as much to do up the servant's room as our own bedroom, shouts the Sailor Boy, stamping his foot like Rumpelstiltzkin. His race—that customary youthful race towards the highest ideals, climbing lamp-posts, Long live the Republic, open-necked shirt, dreams of murdering his father—is run; the last of his contemporaries to do so, he has entered the straight of the home run, made the lightning decision just in time and started running in the opposite direction, became a businessman, renewed all his contacts with wealthy school friends from the Schotten College, bought a hat and yellow pigskin gloves, and punctually every Friday soon after 6 p.m. he arrives at the villa of the industrialist Knapp junior, in Döbling, to play bridge.

There is still one room left, like the mysterious room in the fairy tale which the Princess is not supposed to enter until her twenty-first birthday, left unfurnished, untouched by Frischherz. We'll tackle that later, say the sailor couple, perhaps it will be a library-cum-study, or perhaps a nursery, we'll ask your advice, Bruno, when there's a bit of money in the kitty again.

It is not only in fairy tales that you find objects endowed with souls, conversing, gossiping, making decisions, exuding hatred or affection, living in fact almost like forms of life related to man and the higher animals—sea anemones, perhaps, or proboscidiferous beetles, blowflies too, or moles, wagtails, elephants, and finally myself, the crowning achievement. Spiritualists, too, know about all that—no wonder, a medium is a person, not a thing.

What I'm getting at is the oppressive question, take the beds for example : do the walnut-brown beds in the Advocate's apartment, the mock-German, mock-Gothic carved conjugal beds in the Neighbour's apartment, and the low white steel beds here speak a common bed-language? The sleepers they harbour are closely related, the Neighbour with the Sailor Boy's wife in the most simple, transparent, clear relationship: Father-daughter; just as simple, genealogically speaking, as the line of descent from Advocate father to Sailor Boy son. Why should relations be more complicated between parental beds and children's beds, children's beds, moreover, that are virtually parents' beds again? Nevertheless, the son never wants to lie on the bed his father made, he wants to be free for the murderous old game, break up father's watch-chain, throw father's stiff collar on the floor, grind your heel on it, draw a moustache on the studio portrait of the old man—curtain-raiser and rehearsal for adult life. Join the opposition party in politics; turn businessman if your father is a doctor, an atheist scholar if he is a theologian; become a doctor if father is in business; a solid citizen if father is a charming Jack of all trades, and a Jack of all trades if he is a solid citizen; hence the contrast in beds. Ornamentation is a crime, the plain rod frame of the beds demolishes all those carved knobs, polished grooves, curved headposts of the Old German Gothic bedsteads, glossy white lacquer drives out the old grained and varnished wood: Stifter's *Witiko*, or *Die Mappe meines Urgrossvaters.** Who can stand the wordiness of those old writers! Take it away! Hail, Bright Young Things!

Why does the great Sigmund F.— never actually made a Professor, but true patriarch of souls from the Berggasse, Ninth District (only ten minutes on foot from the Schottenring apartment, should one need his ministrations)—never touch upon these matters? Isn't that a cultural neurosis massing like a great thundercloud above the Neighbour's high, creaking, fake-Gothic double beds? An ankle-low,

* *Die Mappe meines Urgrossvaters*=My Great-Grandfather's Album.

steel-tube bed makes them look criminals, they'll finish up in the Dorotheum Pawnbrokers' and Auction-Rooms, founded by the Emperor Joseph for the benefit of the poor, they'll be labelled fair game and knocked down to the highest bidder among the tatty junk dealers; all the work of the industrious turner, the knob-maker's art, the carpenter's skilled veneering, the Old German soul, Bayreuth, German Gothic, the heart's blood of an art-loving monk, teachers dreaming of a great, Charlemagne-great past, it all goes for nothing, auctioned off, sold for a song, dishonoured.

Pity these works of human hands, highly valued in their time and now despised: the lace gown of the Flower Carnival Queen from the Prater Main Concourse—now just a yellowed rag; Franz Ferdinand's uniform, stained with the blood of Sarajevo—a creased exhibit in the Imperial War Museum; decorations For Valour, patents of nobility rolled up in violet velours—I have a bid, any more? Going—going—gone! I hope that neither Frischherz, nor Sailor Boy, nor Sailor Boy's wife will ever hear that voice of judgment call for the third time, knocking down their snow-white, gloss-painted, uncluttered-line conjugal beds, excommunication of an object that to them is still free from sin.

Three-way involvement of beds: Sailor Boy was conceived in the grained-wood period beds, the Neighbour's daughter was born in the mock-German Gothic carved beds, what will happen now in the snow-white steel-tubing beds, and what will be the consequences?

A new bed, a railside cot, at first put up in the parents' bedroom, further complicates the situation.

No one likes to be a prisoner. To lie behind the rails of a cot, at the mercy of the Mendelian Laws of Heredity, unable to adjust focus to distance or close-up, exposed to the surrounding space like an astronaut, the nursery self bossed about by midwife, mother, nurse, doctors and grandmothers, is a fate which even the infant conceived in an ornament-free bed without a stain cannot escape. Surrounding objects assume the inevitability of fate, circling the cot like the debris of a space flight around the rocket module.

The gaze of the infant self whimpering behind bars takes in nothing at first. The white beds of the parents, the polished wooden beds of the grandparents, the bookcase of first editions, the silk-shaded light with the red rose-hip knob, the fake Chinamen of the apartment next door and the skating Dutchmen at the *Neueste Stern*, the seat cushion with the Chinese reed landscape and the biscuit bust of the young Emperor Franz Joseph, the upright piano with its ensnaring pedals and the grand piano with black-ice surface, the drawing-room chairs and great-grandfather's bed-bench, even the picture postcard of the miracle-working Virgin of Maria Zell and the cookery book with a recipe for soup with liver dumplings, all revolve significantly yet distantly as the planets in a horoscope round the whimpering angry red I in the dropside-cot jail, which can recognise nothing at close-quarters and even less at a distance, but fortunately It does not know. That is why childhood is rightly known as the happiest days of your life.

4 Kitchen Epilogue

Is there no single room in these apartments where the tyranny of inanimate objects is kept at bay? The freedom of the intellect, equal rights for animate beings, could perhaps start in the kitchen.

The gas cooker with its oven belly, from which blue flame spurts out explosively when you light it in the morning, looks just the same inside the *Neue Stern* or the *Neueste*, in the Advocate's apartment or the one designed by Frischherz. The fuel is stored by the Local Authority in leviathan gasometer domes on the far side of the Danube, thence to issue, hissing, not only into the gas lamps of the Ringstrasse but into all these identical-twin gas cookers. They stand in all the bourgeois apartments, and also in the kitchens of Schmölzer, Dr Friedenthal, Frau Kobčiwa, the Schottenring house caretaker—without any class distinctions whatsoever: tin monuments, gas-heated Druid stones, enamelled memorials to the fraternity and positively pre-biblical equality of their owners.

If only families could live as they did in prehistoric Europe, in the Vienna of the Hallstatt period, permanently gathered round their fires. If only they had never escaped into complicated apartments, drawing-rooms, bedrooms, nurseries, bathrooms and studies, then there would be no involved bed genealogies, no Class War between upright and grand pianos, no reason to dread the number 24 within the bourgeois hierarchy of chairs. Life would be as simple as some prehistoric works of art—a sooty handprint on the wall of the living-eating-sleeping cave.

But here the situation does not seem hopeless even now, when I think of the warm oil, sweet egg-and-breadcrumbed Sunday smell of Wiener Schnitzel, floating impartially above the cookers of the Neighbour and the Sailor Boy and the latter's parents, always with the same sated intensity. The savoury scent of parsley on delicately buttered new potatoes and the sweet-and-sour fruity smell of cucumber salad dusted with red pepper rising out of the salad bowls—when I think of all that, I feel that the Class War in the Vienna of the Red Municipal Administration after the fall of the multiracial Empire (gas is readily supplied even to the cookers of the old outlawed aristocracy) has been done away with in a universally pleasing leitmotiv of the kitchen symphony.

Of course that doesn't hold only for Wiener Schnitzel. Special Viennese beef dishes like *Tafelspitz* with horseradish, *Hiefer-Scherzel* or *Dicker Spitz*, are part of a language which everyone in Vienna understands. Why, then, tussle with Grimm's *Dictionary*, or fret over the subtleties, the linguistic hair-splitting of the Duden? Take the *Viennese Cookery Book* of the independent gentlewoman Anna Hofbauer, published in 1825 by Mörschner & Jasper at Kohlmarkt No. 25: in the introduction to the chapter 'Concerning Beef', the well-stewed grammar of the *Tafelspitz* language is already so perfectly worked out that any man of insight can only wonder why the supreme war-lord, His Apostolic Majesty, did not on the spot discard the wretched language regulations—bureaucratic German for God and the Emperor—and graciously consent to introduce the *Tafelspitz* language, which after all everybody from Budweis to Trieste, from Czernowitz to Bludenz, from the

Enns and March to the Pruth, would instinctively understand.

Historians and politicians, like rabbits mesmerised by a snake, have confined their studies to battles, tribes, races, national languages. If only they had reached instead for Anna Hofbauer's *Cookery Book* and, like me, read through the introduction to 'Concerning Beef' about the palate language of *Tafelspitz*, or even *Hiefer-Scherzel* or *Dicker Spitz*, we should have been spared much suffering. The simple housewife Anna Hofbauer of Vienna had, so to speak, a national treasure concealed in her earthenware casserole, and she had begun to fry such a wonderfully fragrant grammar of the palate. . . . But no statesman ever understood the true value of it, though he was glad enough to indulge in the products of her imagination.

> . . . In stewing or slow simmering, to tenderise the meat is not the sole purpose. One must also think of preparing a good strong gravy at the same time, to serve as a sauce for the meat, for the concentrated gravy which frequently collects under the stewed meat often makes the best of sauces without any further additions, and even where additives are found necessary this gravy must in every case form the foundation for the sauce, so that its flavour may harmonise with that of the meat. Consequently nothing could be more foolish than to prepare a separate sauce for stewed or braised meat, as the German cookery books all too frequently advise.

It is unfortunately too late to save the multiracial Empire with my belated recognition of the *Tafelspitz* language. Let us hope it may at least benefit the subsequent republics. Let us hope that in those republics the Minister for Education and Culture may become aware of what it means to have a common palate and *Tafelspitz* language uniting all classes. But will the Permanent Secretary in charge of this department be able to stimulate his appetite at the right moment with some of the wonderfully rich native literature in this language?

A cornucopia filled with cabbage soup, liver dumplings, Salzburg dumplings, Sachertorte, goulash soup, larded leg of venison, plum turnovers and poppyseed buns, small and large plaited loaves, sugared bun loaf, cheese buns, Danish cheese pastry, yeast ring, and freshly baked miniature rolls, flour and semolina from the most renowned mills, as gold letters—like the titles of poems—proclaim on the gold-rimmed black glass sign to right and left of the entrance to the master bakery of Eduard Mang, Vienna III, Salesiangasse, opposite the birth-place of Hugo von Hofmannsthal. Oh, these apocalyptic dreams of a world of blazing soufflé pancakes, quenched with stewed plums! We are such stuff as dreams are made on. . . . How could a bureaucrat recognise this as the sole remaining pillar of the Establishment? A man who probably never pored with burning eyes over Anna Hofbauer's *Cookery Book*, thinking to himself: All theories about the State, from Plato to Kelsen, are not even so much apple sauce, compared with this. . . .

However, class differences, even in the kitchens, are by no means permanently waived even by this language. There is still the question of how often the dishes mentioned appear on the menu. In Schmölzer's kitchen, for example, a crisp Schnitzel only appears on Sundays, at the Neighbour's it may be served more than once a week, in the Advocate's kitchen you could have it every day, but there is always *Tafelspitz* or mince loaf with red cabbage to ring the changes. It may happen that in Schmölzer's kitchen the palate language does not require its meat vocabulary for weeks at a stretch, cabbage and potatoes ruling undisputed. But even a complete command of Vienna's language of the palate would not stop Schmölzer from starting a revolution—as we have seen.

To channel off the cabbage smell into the palaces, and let some of it flow into more modest advocates' apartments, and to preach words of the flesh—not in any sinful sense, purely in the cookery book sense—in Schmölzer's kitchen could be the way to a true Esperanto of the palate, uniting all classes and all nations: towards a language not only understood by everyone, but in everyone's mouth. However, man does not live by meat alone, as my epicurean scripture teacher used to say, he also needs bread to mop up the gravy, so let it be the bread of the spirit.

How can one acquire this bread which has nothing to do with earthly wheat-dust, how can one find such things amid the chaos of indigestible objects: mock-German, mock-Gothic furniture and ornaments, upright pianos and conjugal beds, torn between apartment labyrinths and one-room, kitchen-*kabinett* apartments, kitchens smelling of duck and kitchens smelling of cabbage? It doesn't seem easy to stock this special bread—not an article of everyday use—to get hold of it and appease one's hunger with it. I have not yet discovered it anywhere between Schottenring and Favoriten. Perhaps I shall find it somewhere else. Even Escoffier, that great philosopher of the palate, did not fall from heaven into the kitchen of the Ritz Hotel. He too had to learn, and in the same way I myself, in the kitchen as elsewhere, have by no means completed my search for an ultimate purpose.

5 The Nursery Self

Does it create its own setting or is an apartment setting made for it?

Well, a bit of both. For the moment the Nursery Self is not concerned with apartment settings like those of the Advocate-apartment grandparents next door, or the *Neueste Stern* grandparents in the suburb, or the ornament-free parental apartment. These places are comparable with the blue dots on a map of the Gobi Desert, blue like the waters of the oases, which are very rare. But if the Nursery Self is lucky, It will eventually reach the blue oases, the settled positions.

At present It is in a sort of pre-Socratic position, which It did not create and which was not created for It, it was all just there, like the Mendelian Laws of Heredity. Everything just flows, milk flows, urine and saliva flow, the world is an oral and anal paradise and the rivers of paradise flow for ever. . . .

The corners and edges of the room, even the cot-rails, are mere shadows to the infant eye. Sucking milk is merely a reflex action essential to survival, yet nevertheless this is where trouble starts.

My Infant Self sucks milk which (leaving the feeble trickle of mother's milk aside) comes not from far-off holy cows, let alone from mooncalves grown up into mooncows, but from the dairy at the corner of Schottenring and Börsengasse, having been stored in the udders of large brown-and-white cows somewhere between Anninger and Tulbinger Kogel, milked by a Lower Austrian milkmaid into a pail, put into tin milk cans at the roadside, collected by the lorry of the Milk Marketing Co-operative, delivered to the Vienna Central Dairy owned by the Municipal Authority, there to be sterilised under the supervision of a medical officer of the City of Vienna. Released as Babymilk in special bottles, transported by night in jolting (still horse-drawn) milk carts whose iron wheels clatter over Vienna's granite roads between two and four every morning to the dairy at the corner of Schottenring and Börsengasse. Fetched by my grandmother's maid, who is called either Maria or Resi, warmed for me, filled into my bottle and put to the polyp-greedy sucker of my mouth.

The suckling set-up is exceedingly dangerous, not made by the Infant Self and not made for It, simply there, like the Mendelian Laws or the conditioned reflex salivating of the severed head in one of Pavlov's dog experiments. Think of all the things I am ingesting, hapless Infant Self, together with the sterilised milk of my native city.

One can move out of apartments. Dusty cut-glass chandeliers can be taken to the junk dealer in Leopoldstadt; mock-German, mock-Gothic conjugal beds can be sold at a small loss; divan cushions with embroidered windmills can be given away, even old bedding can be got rid of. Take it to the Dorotheum, the State pawnbrokers, get a loan from Auntie Dorothy, and just never redeem the stuff. Laughing fake Chinamen can, if the worst comes to the worst, be thrown into the Danube Canal, in the reasonable hope that the Danube will carry them down to the Bosphorus alongside the boulders. But the milk intake always leaves some residue.

A bottle of milk every four hours, milk that has passed through the bottling plant of the proudly socialist Central Dairy of the City of Vienna. Isn't the helpless Nursery Self bound at the same time to absorb that community's humane desire to dispense happiness—that fierce devotion to the welfare of war orphans, consumptive labourers, mutilated building workers, pupils of the deaf-and-dumb institution, rachitic technical college students, semi-literate frequenters of public libraries, boil-ridden users of public baths and night-club tarts longing to reform—always with the battle-cry 'The rich must pay'?

What a warring assortment of vitamin complexes in this apparently harmless bottle of Babymilk! I see that from the first moment of my cot existence I was placed in such a delicate political situation that it is hard or even impossible to say who was to blame. I don't know that I even want to ferret it out, though I could certainly embarrass my father with the slogan 'Procreation means Guilt'. But that would besmirch my mother's name as well, and a hapless Nursery Self in this exposed political situation needs mother love that can grow with It, unclouded by doubts about life.

As yet, the unsteady Lilliputian perception machine can hardly perceive very much as It gropes Its way around the objects. Take the low-slung white-lacquered tubular-steel beds of the parents: easy to climb up on, It will decide, but their symbolic aspect—low beds of tubular steel as a protest and warning against the old-fashioned beds of shiny walnut next door and the much-carved mock-German, mock-Gothic beds in the suburban apartment—will remain hidden until further notice. A visit to the grandmother next door, even when It is already at the walking stage, opens up no perspectives into the past. In Its eyes she is not a Makart beauty who plays the lute and sings Schubert-lieder, deceives her Jewish Advocate husband with a Roman Catholic naval commodore and had her sons baptised to open all possible doors to success in the multiracial Empire (which, alas, no longer exists).

She is simply a grandmother, who lifts It on to the balcony balustrade to show It a pleasure-steamer decorated with Chinese lanterns, lying at anchor down by the landing-stage on the Danube Canal, slowly crusting over with pleasure-bent ant-people, red, green, blue and yellow lights coming up on the chains of garlands leading from the funnel to prow and stern, and, as the music springs up like a breeze on the steamer's deck and the ship casts off from the landing-stage, she says: 'Look, that's going to Nussdorf!'

Or take the lift. For It, that is not a thing in which domesticated witches without brooms, accompanied by sedate thunder and creaking of steel cables, rise up the lift-shaft like civic blood corpuscles to the fourth or the sixth floor, to leave the magic circulation again as a model, or a client, or a patient, an articled clerk or a baron, according to which storey they get out on.

That is Its diving-bell which It enters with Its nurse, the maid will crank it down to Ringstrasse level, to caretaker's cat level. Large black caretaker's tomcat, sitting on the polished shelf outside the glass window of the porter's lodge from which his master dispenses information like the Delphic Oracle, strictly according to mood and tip rendered: Herr Baron is away on holiday, Herr Doctor has already left this morning, the young gentleman is not yet back for lunch, you can leave registered letters with me. The tomcat arches his black hump, plays with his tomcat claws, stretches and grows as large and imposing as the bearded, winged gatekeeper animals at the Temple of Baalbek. Then, possibly, he remembers that in this bourgeois Ringstrasse house there are no eternal treasures of divine origin to be guarded, and deflates again to the size of a porter's black tom—but for It, carried by, or led by the hand of, Its nurse, on the way from the lift diving-bell to the caryatid-guarded entrance, the creature does have the grandeur of a bearded, winged, gatekeeper monster, half-beast, half-caretaker, at the Temple of Baalbek.

Or take the carpet, the fake Persian, in the grandmother's drawing-room : unlike Its father, It does not see this as a flypaper on which ladies are cruelly trapped after a tea-party to hear the lady of the house sing Schubert. Nor as a dust-catching monstrosity, which—as Bruno Frischherz explains to the Sailor Boy's wife—with its unauthentic, industrially manufactured colours just sets off the glass cabinet with laughing porcelain Chinamen, the beribboned lute and the piano with its gold-tasselled velvet cover, to perfection. Rather, the carpet is a soft playground, on which a swift-flying ball, trundling over the maze pattern at the edge, comes to rest; a red-green-and-blue-mottled felt pasture on which It can crawl without having to put Its hands on cold parquet; a soft piece of roomscape, on which the black trunks of piano legs grow, above which the underside of the table forms a rough wooden sky, and in the evening the cut-glass chandelier—which by day is a glockenspiel, its cut-glass rhomboids clinking against one another with every draught—rises like a drawing-room sun, turning the landscape into a Promised Land.

The Nursery Self is well on the way to finding Its bearings. Who knows in what manner It would have discovered the grandfather's carved office desk, the antlered clothes-stand in the office lobby, the cook's rose-red basic featherbed cover, and the bust of a young and handsome Emperor Franz Joseph, had not the parents decided to move away, out into the Green Belt.

6 The Holiday Scene, or the Idyllic Summer-House

The move to the Green Belt is effected via a move to verdant Styria, where a summer-house is taken, in which one stays put for two months to gather strength for the winter.

The true value of a cure at a spa or a summer holiday, says the wife of the Imperial and High Court Advocate, Grandmother of the Cot Persona, is only revealed at Christmas. How you feel at Christmas will show how well or ill you planned your holidays.

Uncles and aunts, sisters and cousins, and her very nearest and dearest, have to listen to this all through autumn, winter and spring. When someone asks, Where shall we go this summer, they discover how deeply the Calvinist harshness of even a secularised belief in predestination has entered the soul of this Imperial and High Court Advocate's wife, though she may enjoy singing Schubert-lieder, has a tender-looking mouth, and is in fact of Jewish origin. They discover that the choice of spa or holiday resort may be left to you, but in any case you won't know until Christmas how your choice turned out. Whether you did, in fact, restore, refresh, regenerate, revive yourself, whether the fresh strength the doctor ordered was duly collected.

In the circumstances—every summer turning out ineluctably fateful—it is hardly surprising that no one cared to risk a suggestion, or even raise the customary objections : I think that in Carinthia the weather is more reliable than in the Salzkammergut—you get more sun perhaps; I hear Marienbad is a bit cheaper than Carlsbad. Does the whole family always have to stay in the same place? Couldn't the younger ones go on a cruise for a change, from Trieste to Ragusa for example?

Not a bit of it. They were all terrorised by the thought of next Christmas. Undoubtedly they will turn out to have made the wrong decision, because they feel ill, or they don't feel anything in particular, and it is as though the summer holiday had never been, and all that good money was spent for nothing.

In the end the choice is invariably left to her, the Sailor Boy's mother. No wonder, nobody wants to stick his neck out, and she invariably decides on Lake Grundl. A peculiar choice, because it nearly always rains there, Salzburger 'strip' rain. Editors of local papers make this phenomenon the subject of leading articles, it reaches the columns of the most famous newspapers in Hamburg, Frankfurt and Berlin, even (in the form of a reader's letter) the London *Times*.

My grandmother knows all that. Also the difficulties of the journey: by Western Railway from Vienna West Station, with my cot taken to pieces, via St Pölten, St Valentin, St Rhythm-of-the-wheels, to Linz and Attnang-Puchheim. So far so good. But then the change at Attnang-Puchheim, with child's cot, suitcases, hatboxes, nappie basket, daughter-in-law and daughter-in-law's parents! The worker, and how much more so the worker's representative, has an equal right, a legal right at that, to go on holiday. One should not grudge him these bourgeois appurtenances.

Mind you, Sailor Boy himself has stayed behind in Vienna, he will come on later. He cannot stand family picnics, family outings, family departures, family processions in general.

At Attnang-Puchheim you change on to the tiny Salzkammergut line, whose carriages smell of axle-grease and cheap floor-polish, whose seats are wooden benches and which shake like ox-carts, and it's another two hours to Bad Aussee—but it's already raining, and the drops beat incessantly on the tin roof of the carriage, like a hail of chickpeas. There must be reasons for all this, over and above my grandmother's passion for trout fishing—which is hardly ever crowned with success, although she wanders along the banks of the swift-flowing Traun in a most expensive lady angler's outfit, the green trout basket strapped over her shoulder, casting her trout-fly, making it hop and skip over the green Traun water, reeling in, casting, reeling in, again and again with no success. Then she changes over to the gravelly shore of Lake Grundl, changes the fly for a worm, sits down on a landing-stage and confines herself to catching minnows. Minnows are easier to catch than trout, but they are full of bones and nobody wants to eat them. So that can't be the reason for going to Lake Grundl. Nor can the weather, as I have indicated.

Perhaps it's the house: a greyish-brown wooden house with orange-red, butterfly-yellow, cloud-white begonias flowering in the green-painted window-boxes, and shutters with a heart cut out at the centre. The woodman, or 'wood and forestry labourer' in the officialese of the State Forestry Commission, Röberl-Hans, commonly known as Weg-Hansl—his true name is only used in the baptismal register and on his call-up papers when there is a war—built this wooden house for himself. In summer he rents it to holiday-makers, trout fishermen, minnow fishermen, mushroom gatherers, alpine ramblers, Sunday huntsmen, alpine tourists, raspberry pickers, azalea gatherers. He built it by the sweat of his brow—like Adam toiling outside the gates of Eden—after work and on Sundays and holidays. He got the wood for building from the Crown forests, partly free, partly at reduced price, and above all he felled it himself, drove it down to the valley on the wooden sledge over the icy snow-crust (and you can tell how often that has ended in disaster, from the crosses beside the wood tracks: Meierl-Xaver on 10th January—the year is eroded away—together with the woodcutters Moser and Steinegger, went down to the valley on the wood sledge. He got under the sledge and died in the twenty-seventh year of his life. Say an Our Father for him). That is what can happen. However, Röberl-Hans managed to build his house, and his wife Marianne dragged tubs of gravel up from the shore of the lake for the garden paths. This activity, as the Vicar of Bad Aussee will regretfully inform you, apparently strained the ligaments of her reproductive apparatus—which seems to have been a disadvantage during the birth of her first child.

However, the doctors' and lawyers' wives from Vienna, the Imperial and State councillors, the Burgtheater actors, both active and retired, the sons of the *haute bourgeoisie* who walk around the lake in *lederhosen*, don't come to Styria to probe into the building problems of Röberl-Hans or the gynaecological complications of his wife Marianne. To go into such problems, which are pretty much the same in towns, one could perfectly well stay in Vienna, order one's third, or even one's fourth, black coffee in the Café Herrenhof and go on talking, take up the consulting hours of the popular and famous gynaecologists and psychiatrists, as usual, and occasionally, also as usual, discuss with one's bank manager the chances of a loan in view of a future legacy. Similar life games as those of Röberl-Hans, though with higher stakes and more difficult rules: the whole thing more impenetrable and confused, like a classical ballet, still performed as arranged by the great Petipa, which has got into a muddle on a modern revolving stage, as compared with a simple alpine comic song meant to alert the sleeping peasant girl to the possibilities of the night which has just begun.

Of course, the passionate attachment of the young writer Jakob Tataruga (his father, Dr Bruno Tataruga, collects folk-lore and for two generations has owned a summer-house by Lake Grundl—to wit, the 'Villa Tataruga') to Isa, the still attractive wife of a senior civil servant from the Ministry of Education and Culture on the Minoriten Square in Vienna, could be compared with the premarital relations, traditional in these parts, of Röberl-Hans with his native Marianne. It is love, after all, in both cases. The cry of 'Back to Nature' would long ago have drowned in the noise of all those Fiats and Daimlers and Tatras, had not the wives of doctors and lawyers, the councillors and civil servants, current and retired Burgtheater actors, as well as the sons of the *haute bourgeoisie* trying to be writers, unanimously decided, signed, sealed and delivered, now and for all time, that the living and loving of the Noble Savages in the mountains of Styria are enacted according to better, stronger, purer as well as more full-blooded laws than our own; they *must* obey better, stronger, purer as well as more full-blooded laws. That is why we come here, at the best time of the year between 1st July and 1st September, to this 'wonderful, heart-warming landscape, with those good people in it', to quote Frau Tataruga.

Then again there is always a possibility that in the middle of a wood, looking for mushrooms or picking berries, or angling for trout by the swift-flowing Traun or elsewhere, one may, unexpectedly and without previous introduction, run into a Count Meran or a Count Kesselstatt, in black *lederhosen* with green leaves embroidered thereon, coat of *loden* and goat's beard hat, a hessian huntsman's bag slung over his shoulder, iron-tipped hazelwood mountaineering-stick in his right hand, quite casually on an outcrop of rock, on a grassy saddle between two stone-grey mountain peaks, or even on the footpath between Bad Aussee and Lake Grundl.

Just think, he looks exactly like Röberl-Hans. Watch the noble count—whose father took part in the Imperial Hunt at Bad Ischl, beyond the Pötschenpass, struck the finest deer dead in the shoulder with a perfect shot—vanish among hazel bushes, raspberry thickets and dwarf pines, not before he has said a friendly *'Grüss Gott'*. One might meet a Princess Hohenlohe, too, in a similar way, not usually wearing *lederhosen* once she is above flapper age, but in a rose-red dirndl skirt, with green bodice, white puff sleeves and striped dirndl apron.

They might have gone on for another thousand years in full possession of all their titles and privileges, ambling from one alpine pasture to another in the summer, affably saying *'Grüss Gott'*, saving all their intrigues for the winter season at the Court of Vienna. But the pestilential carriers of the freedom epidemic, those sons of professors and advocates, and later on the damnable Schmölzers and their comrades, dissolved the Holy Roman Empire of the German people piecemeal, as the miners do the salt-bearing rocks in the saline distillery in Bad Aussee, in a great seething mixture, and stirred it all up with their democratic rods, until the democratic salt settled out. Now everyone has to take a pinch of this salt between his fingers, and not one bread roll in the Republic, from Lake Constance to Lake Neusiedler, can escape being oversalted thereby. Perhaps the good old Emperor Franz Joseph in his summer villa in Bad Ischl might have staved off disaster that little bit longer, had he not, refractory as an old councillor about to retire, knowing that nothing more can possibly happen to him, insisted on going about all summer in *lederhosen* and *loden* coat, Styrian hat with chamois brush and a green hunter's bag. He would not be dissuaded from chasing stags, deer and chamois thus got up in the costume of Röberl-Hans—or of the Counts Meran and Kesselstatt. Why couldn't he occasionally wear the handsome embroidered uniform of a Hungarian nobleman, or the red-embroidered, snow-white linen dress of a Croatian peasant, for the Imperial chase? It might have saved us a lot of misery.

But perhaps after all he was not as much to blame as the universally popular Archduke Johann. Why did *he* have to fall in love with the unaristocratic postmaster's daughter Anna Plochl, marry her despite the opposition of the Court and make her into the Countess Meran? Why did he too wander among the alpine meadows dressed up as a Styrian huntsman in leather shorts and coat and sit down unrecognised, or at any rate without announcing who he was, in alpine huts with the dairymaids, eating bread soup and oxtails along with them, his greatest pleasure in being accepted as a non-archduke? At such moments a word of praise from his Commander-in-Chief would have meant less to him than a dairymaid asking him in Styrian accents: 'And who might you be?'

Undoubtedly the affability of the highborn left its mark on the local population, or, as Frau Tataruga puts it, pointing out a particularly fine figure of a woodman with a

Roman nose, passing by in his *loden* coat: 'One wouldn't mind the Archduke Johann in one's own family tree, incognito or otherwise!'

The *loden* coat in these parts, like the Madonna's sheltering mantle, covers high and low alike—Count Meran or Röberl-Hans—and it can be as grey as the sheer rock face or as green as the alpine meadows around Lake Langang. It keeps rain off the regional costume—indeed, it is equally impermeable to all the storms in the contemporary sky. A *loden* coat is like a knight's suit of armour (even in a republic); which would also keep out news of economic and stock-market depression in America, reports of secretive, inhuman laws passed by neighbouring dictatorships, and comments from the Anglo-Saxon press about peasants starving in the Ukraine or political murders in Russia. When the *loden* coat gets really wet, it is hung on the wooden rails above the stove—and by the next morning it is completely dry again.

The secrets of *loden* and the pedigree of well-grown timbermen or of the Counts Meran, or the—to my mind—deplorable political effects of *lederhosen* worn at the Imperial Hunt, or the passionate enthusiasm of Viennese doctors' and lawyers' wives, councillors and civil servants, active and retired Burgtheater actors, as well as the sons, would-be writers, of the *haute bourgeoisie* looking for the Noble Savage in the mountains of Styria—one might call that the Bourgeois Hunt, as opposed to the Imperial Hunt, which hunts actual wild animals instead of Noble Savages—one needs to be as conversant with all this as Frau Tataruga or my grandmother to understand fully the joy and the sense of drama that accompany the re-entry every summer into the modest woodman's house, where one doesn't miss urban comforts. The brown wooden veranda is the gateway to the Röberl house, with orange-red, butterfly-yellow, cloud-white begonias in the window-boxes, and four-colour prints hanging in rustic carved frames: roaring stags in autumnal woods, a wan moon above a clearing, two poachers and a gamekeeper, the gamekeeper confronts one poacher with the illegally slain deer, while the second poacher, concealed in the background, aims his gun at the gamekeeper, thus neatly disposing of four lives in one go. The wooden veranda is also the repository for wooden clogs—the natives only enter the house in special socks which have a felt sole sewn on; and breakfast is served there.

Through this wooden gateway lies the path of the Grandmother, the Neighbour and his wife, the path of their daughter, and the airborne path of my Nursery Self (I still get carried, though I am certainly beginning to harbour dark thoughts about this sudden disagreeable change of venue right at the best time of year) into the kitchen/living-room. On the stove sits a tomcat, black as the caretaker's cat in the Schottenring house in Vienna. That just goes to show how life needs a change of characters and scenes to bring out its shape. Look at the Schottenring tom and the Styrian tom, both black, both able to purr, to extend and retract their claws, yet they live in different worlds—two simple tomcat lives are as different as the life of Confucius from that of a Styrian poacher.

The Schottenring tom sees, instead of mice, a succession of articled clerks, clients, patients, barons and other Ringstrasse types, animals too large for him to catch, he has to cringe in front of them. Instead of watching a mousehole, he sits in front of the porter's lodge, only half an animal—not surprising, really—the other half a caretaker.

The Styrian tom frequently leaps down from the stove to the kitchen floor, glides across the wooden veranda, out through the hole beside the veranda door, and then with one bound he has a whole world of meadows and woods full of mouseholes at his disposal. No wonder that he often returns to the kitchen with a dead fieldmouse between his teeth and lays the little brownish-yellow corpse at the feet of my grandmothers—don't forget that the Neighbour's wife is also my grandmother and also here on holiday—or my mother. And they all pull their dirndl skirts up and cry for help to Röberl-Hans.

Of course the kitchen is not furnished solely as a tom-cat's domicile. A square wooden table seating eight, hemmed in on two sides by the fumed oak corner bench, serves for the feeding of humans. Where the two back-planks of the bench meet there is a small crack, as in porous rock; a wooden cross hangs there, underneath is a small shelf with a spray of azaleas in a pottery vase, or alpine primulas, or gentian, or just dwarf conifer twigs, according to the time of year. 'God's corner' here is a place for flowers rather than a proper shrine. Just as the local priest is a christenings, marriages and deaths priest, not a spiritual village king as among the wealthy peasants of the Inn district or the Tyrol.

The woodmen hereabouts, says the Neighbour, are rural proletarians, good comrades, and don't you forget that. The unruly Protestants in Goisern and Hallstatt at the time of the Counter-Reformation, how did they manage to survive here, how did they avoid the immigrant fate of the Salzburg Protestants,* never giving up, never losing the spirit of opposition? The Neighbour regards the Counter-

* The Salzburg Protestants fled from the Counter-Reformation and settled in the Mark Brandenburg around Berlin.

Reformation as a Spanish Civil War veteran does fascism —and of course he has a perfect right to do so. Spirit of opposition and never give up—still, perhaps it makes for a healthier summer holiday to follow Frau Tataruga's advice : 'I'm always telling my husband not to go on about politics amidst all this wonderful unspoilt Nature!'

The sideboard of pinewood completes the kitchen inventory. It hasn't been mentioned before, although it stands to the left of the entrance, the top being a dresser for plates and glasses and tin lids, and for tall cylindrical coffee-mugs with inscriptions like 'A present from Gmunden', 'A Present from Bad Ischl', 'A Present from Old-Aussee'—why not 'A Present from Rio', the best coffee surely comes from Brazil? The lower part has drawers for tin plates and cups, saucepans, cooking spoons, cutlery and chopping board.

What about water? The cold pure mountain spring-water comes out of the rock above the treeline, runs down grassy slopes past low-growing gentians, makes a good nursery for young trout, heals wounded deer (as Parson Kneipp* so rightly observed in the last century), drives rattling mill-wheels, and finally feeds the green lake with cold pure mountain spring-water. A large watering can is filled from the wooden butt in front of the house and put on a small oilcloth-covered table beside the stove.

The remaining rooms of the Röberls' wooden house have two wooden beds apiece—excepting the attic with its sloping ceiling, where there is only room for one—also a table, no bigger than a breakfast tray, an armchair, and a wash-stand with a large cream-coloured china wash-bowl whose base is painted with sprays of flowers and leaves.

* Advocate of the Kneipp 'Water Cure'.

Pour cold water from the bulging china ewer : the china flowers grow moist and seem to expand like Japanese paper flowers, which in a glass of water burst from the pellets, everting green paper stalks like fish fins, unroll artificial blossoms like geishas' paper parasols. I can make such a world of magic flowers for myself here : immerse my hands in water to pulse-level, keep still and wait for sunbeams which sometimes dart like dragonflies over the submerged china flower world and vanish behind a green china tendril—keep my hot hands still for a long time in cold water, stare as though frozen at the magically glowing china flower garden, whose luminosity wanes as the water gradually warms up. Moving the hands destroys the Asiatic flower world, buries it under waves in the china wash-bowl. So swiftly can the loveliest man-made landscape perish : a slight movement of the hands; so swiftly did I return to the reality of the austere room in the wooden house.

What else is worth mentioning besides the wooden bed, table and chair, china bowl and ewer? The simple built-in wooden cupboard perhaps, or the jars of jam on its protruding top edge. Marianne Röberl picks raspberries, strawberries, bilberries and cranberries all summer long and preserves them for the winter or for next year, and puts the jars on top of the cupboard. It is also worth mentioning that the widest-ranging and most fantastic of imaginary journeys have taken place in rooms of a spartan simplicity.

Take the dismal classroom of my grammar school. There was a smell of cheap floor-polish, which seeped like a black slug-trail over the floorboards, the low wooden benches ink-stained, carved and bitten by generations of scholars, bare white barrack-room walls, and the photograph of the Head of State in a black official frame, an iron stove looking like an old-fashioned coffee-mill—it was either red-hot as though with rage and the pupils sweated and forgot their Latin verbs, or it was ice-cold and black as a Jesuit of the Inquisition and the pupils froze and scraped their feet along the floor under the benches trying to get warm, and again forgot their Latin verbs. But the imaginary journeys without tickets which started out from these evil-smelling rooms—the range of them!

With Homer from isle to isle of the blue Aegean, with Ovid to the Golden or Silver Age, or to Latin peasants who are really frogs. With King Lear, vanishing in English moorland mists, besieging Valmy with Goethe, or climbing the church tower in Swabia with Mörike to see to the weathercock because it creaks in the wind. In the mathematics lesson, past cube roots, tetrahedrons, trapezia, rhombuses, rhomboids, conical sections, skull-caps and top hats—daydream trips along this trigonometrical mountain range, to the dancing class, which only takes place on Thursdays between 5 and 7 p.m.—the range of them!

Nowadays the schoolboy sits on adjustable, rotating, foam-rubber padded physical culture chairs in fitted-carpet school palaces, will only deign to contemplate the voyage of the Argonauts as a tape recording with genuine Mediterranean wave-sounds, meets his girl friend at 10 o'clock break and shares a fruit juice in maty fashion, leaves his comfortable chair, unjaded, at the fixed time, on the way home buys reefers to smoke in the evening with his girl friend in the students' bar—what a range! O for that bird of paradise, the grammar-school boy's imagination that was! That bird singes his wings on pot and can barely keep airborne in school barrack-rooms no longer smelling of floor-polish—feed on comic strips, bird, or die!

Of course one can also turn one's back on the austere room in the Röberls' wooden house, stand by the window and look at the green lake, a green-ice mirror surface in good weather, cleft twice a day by the white-painted steamer *Rudolf*, drawing the foam crests of the churned-up wake like a wedding-veil, puffing toy smoke-clouds as it passes the rounded pudding protruberance of the Ressenberg. The fir-studded Ressen grows out of the lake, its mossy edges, overgrown with bilberry and cranberry bushes, merging into the light green shore. On that opposite Ressenberg-side of the lake there are no gravel shores or beaches, one can only get there by boat. It has to be made fast to a tree, and then one leaps from the prow straight on to the mossy ruff of the Pudding Mountain. My grandmothers later told me that the Seven Dwarfs lived on this mountain, there was absolutely no doubt that this was their home—however, they never come down to the moss-covered foot of the Pudding Mountain, where our human boats anchor.

But where is the Sailor Boy, father of the Nursery Self, when he visits at weekends, Sundays and Holy Days? He sits in a corner of the wooden veranda, smoking a stumpy English pipe and pursuing thoughts which one might call *Imaginary Folk-Lore Rambles of a Young Pipe-Smoker*.

Look at that old Tataruga for instance, he thinks, passing by in his greasy *lederhosen*, azalea spray on his Styrian hat, a sort of bourgeois shrunk version of the Archduke Johann—going about from dairymaid to dairymaid, extracting from these women of the Alps doggerel verses, old yodelling songs, folk-tunes and ghost stories, to be noted down, correlated, copied, just to make a bigger and better second or third edition of his Life's Work, the *Atlas of Folk Art* in the Aussee Valley, a collection which is already famous. That old Tataruga with his outsize ears—ear trumpets for folk-lore, which he trains on cowmen's huts, peasants' kitchens, woodmen's rooms, shooting-sites, inns and laundries, just as the local doctor lays his polished wood stethoscope on some old peasant's chest.

Green my stockings, green my hat,
Suits my love, I'm sure of that,
And a green hat ribbon too,
Goes together like us two!

And my mother in her *loden*-grey fishing get-up, chasing bony minnows—now wouldn't that make a *loden*-inspired, Styrian-green, alpine yet also spiritual relationship, whereby the white-bearded Jewish fathers and grandfathers, all still brought up in Moravian ghettoes, of these two holiday-makers, would be finally banished from the family tree into the realm of legend. Wonder why those two don't like each other? Perhaps they're too alike. When Dr Tataruga meets my mother fishing for minnows by the end of the lake when he's waiting on the landing-stage in front of Ladner's Inn, for the steamer *Rudolf*, Tataruga just raises his Styrian hat with the goat's beard politely, says '*Küss die Hand*' in a friendly way, and that's all. I'd like to transplant those two into the Karst Mountains, make them water orange trees. I'd make them herd sheep in the Holy Land. If the worst comes to the worst, Dr Tataruga and my mother could teach the small children there to read. Maybe they're a bit too old and unaccustomed to hard physical work. . . . As far as I'm concerned they could even sit beside Mount Tabor doing nothing, except pray perhaps—but liberal bourgeois don't pray, they only worship: Art, or Nature, Beautiful People, Good People, above all the Great Men of Human History, Plato, Dante, Napoleon, even Karl Marx. Or Noble Savages in the

Styrian Mountains and their old songs and tunes, as set down for all time in Tataruga's *Gleanings*.

But reform yourself first, Styrian Sailor Boy. There you sit on the Röberls' veranda, in *lederhosen* and green socks (yours, too, are reinforced with a felt sole), smoking your pipe. Admittedly you were brought up wrong, like everyone else nowadays, by Tataruga, Civil Service minds and a whole flock of sheeplike patriots. Three generations away from the ghetto, with a dip in the font en route—it's like a speeded up express train journey from Lemberg to the Côte d'Azur. Hot Borscht in the evening, and next morning oysters and mimosa shrubs. At last you've achieved a generation that can walk on the Promenade des Anglais in Nice without looking ridiculous; you can meet a Count Meran or a Prince Hohenlohe in the forest thickets of the Styrian Mountains and look almost like one of them in your *loden*-coat and Styrian hat, and then you start going on about the Holy Land again, and want to force your mother, even if it's only in your imagination, into a proletarian army that crawls about on some Karst mountain without knowing what's going to happen. At least your mother and that old Tataruga know what they hope to get out of a summer in the Salzkammergut: minnows from Lake Grundl, and new pages for the *Gleanings*. But what you hope for, as you sit there in *lederhosen* smoking a pipe on the Röberls' veranda, would make both a liberal philanthropist and a progressive colonist thoroughly fed up, it's so vague.

Amid all the *loden* and Styrian hat speculations I almost forgot the Neighbour, who has also moved into the Röberls' house. How does he spend the summer? He doesn't fish, either for trout or minnows, he doesn't collect old folktunes, he is not mad about steamer trips, and politically, too, there is not much to interest him here. Röberl and his woodmen friends may be good old comrades—an aspect rather played down when one chats with bourgeois holiday-makers. But the Socialist Party, as respectable citizens rightly point out, has sunk into bankruptcy. Anyhow, it lost the miniature civil war and the Neighbour has lost his seat in Parliament. He has been compulsorily retired as secretary of the Printers' Union, and did three months in jail as 'a political'—no wonder that he has retreated to a position nobody can take away from him : Back to Nature. And he says with a conviction which everyone who knows anything at all about the interplay of the parties of Left and Right during the fifteen years of the First Republic will readily accept as genuine : More and more do I find that Nature is my true love.

Can all these attitudes be united, not merely in one fir-ringed valley, over which the occasional confused eagle may actually circle, but under one roof?

They can indeed, when Ricki Tedesco gives her famous 'Log Cabin Party'. The log cabin is the great wooden house by the lake. Ricki Tedesco inherited it from her grand-father, Burgtheater actor grandfather, King Lear, Ottokar, Wallenstein and Borodin grandfather,* who often sought Styrian solitude, breathed Styrian air into his actor's lungs to make his Lear even greater in the next theatre season, not to mention his Ottokar, Wallenstein and Borodin.

It was a sight to see, the old tragedian coming for Christmas from Bad Ischl via Goisern and the chamois-steep Pötschenpass, by sledge into the Aussee Valley, wrapped in rugs, a warm brick to left and right of his noble bottom, and a hatbox full of scripts.

*** Ottokar and Borodin are leading characters in plays by Franz Grillparzer; Wallenstein refers to Schiller's trilogy of that name.**

The New Year's Eve parties in his snow-bound wooden house by the lake were so famous that woodmen's children would still be talking about them in summer: telling of fat doughnuts flying out of the chimney soon after midnight (the frying pans being so overfilled with doughnuts that the upward draught of the wood-fire sometimes seizes a batch and slings them out into New Year's Night). Of course the old tragedian was utterly enchanted to hear of this newly created children's legend, with *his* house as the focal point. He immediately dashed off a song with the chorus:

> Then doughnuts on Lake Grundl fall
> Like champagne corks in castle hall.

and sang it to his guests—not that they'd asked him to.

With this well-pensioned Bohemian* in her family tree, the inherited but enlarged wooden house by the lake, a husband who is both banker and industrialist and often away, with that husband's money and her own subtle awareness of the intricate summer social structure of the valley, nothing could be easier or more enjoyable for Ricki Tedesco than to unite all the elements—woodcutting, Styrian, wet-*loden*, aristocratic, bourgeois, left wing, young and old, baptised and unbaptised, mountaineering and trout fishing, holiday-making and native, yodel-gay and town-suit gloomy, inhibited and abandoned, legitimate and illegitimate, educated and uneducated, pure speech and dialect, dairymaid and doctor of philosophy, waitresses at Ladner's Inn and Burgtheater actors, descendants of the Archduke Johann and descendants of the socialist leader

* Burgtheater actors are State employed—with annual increments, State pensions and Civil Service style titles.

from Vienna's Favoriten district—all united that first weekend of August for her 'Log Cabin Party'.

On the log cabin terrace Chinese lanterns are strung up as on the deck of a pleasure-steamer cruising from the Danube Canal Bridge to Nussdorf. The wooden railings bear garlands of fir twigs, trestle tables and seats borrowed from Ladner's Inn, put up a small platform for the woodmen's band, set two barrels of beer on wood blocks, large plates of salami and Extrawurst, Cracow-Wurst, bacon and cheese, bread and sliced hard-boiled eggs, two-litre bottles of red wine at one-metre intervals along the tables, and in the kitchen keep the frying pans of hot fat ready for the 'doughnut barbecue', keeping up the old tragedian's doughnut tradition :

> Then doughnuts on Lake Grundl fall
> Like champagne corks in castle hall.

It's as simple as that, the practical side of Ricki Tedesco's Log Cabin Party : Just a simple country dance at a simple country cottage, says the younger Tataruga mockingly. I hope they'll play only the beautiful old country dances and Styrian airs, says the old Tataruga. Well, just a tango or a foxtrot now and then, says Ricki, you won't grudge us that, Herr Doctor, we won't corrupt your woodmen, of course, by letting them play such stuff, I'll use my record player for that.

The question of dress also more or less answers itself. Moss green, fir green, grass green, strawberry red, raspberry red, azalea rose-pink, plum blue, sky blue, forget-me-not blue—what girl, woman or lady could not find a skirt colour among all these to go with her dirndl bodice and her dirndl apron? If you can't recognise the flora and fauna of our Styrian alpine world in the colour and shape microcosm of our dirndl materials, you must be either blind or an intellectual ne'er-do-well devoid of any feeling for natural beauty. It is easier for the men. They don't have to rummage for days in the regional costume shop at Bad Aussee among the colour and shape microcosm of the Styrian alpine world to find the right thing. For them it's either black *lederhosen* embroidered with greenery, or plain black knee-length *lederhosen*, or full-length *loden* trousers with a double green stripe down each side, or plain brown *lederhosen*. The upper half, too, has only a limited choice: grass-green indigenous jacket with little brown chamois embroidered above the back pleat, or grey *loden* jacket that goes with the grey *loden* trousers with the green double stripe at the side, with stag's horn buttons and green cuffs, pockets and lapels, or simply dance in shirt-sleeves and green waistcoat with silver buttons when it gets too hot—there's no problem.

What actually happens later on at the Log Cabin Party is more of a problem. I don't mean how far yodel-gay females fraternise, as the party mood waxes, with town-suit gloomy males, or vice versa, nor, of course, am I trying to establish how often under Ricki Tedesco's tiled and generous roof the legitimate mingles with the illegitimate, and when bourgeois male and left-wing female disappear together after a Styrian jig among the hazel-nut bushes (which line the brook-bank behind the storage shed) and outhouses of the Tedesco property, I let it pass, although this particular paean of peace does not, to my mind, form a reliable leitmotiv for Class War pacification. Even the not too frequent conjunctions of aristocratic male and bourgeois, or even left-wing female (the combination of aristocratic male and yodel-gay female, sometimes even in its legitimate, but much more often in its illegitimate form, is of course the most frequent here, to the point of splendidly healthy progeny), are merely noted, without revealing further details and without hunting down such side branches in the family trees of the native woodmen's families, Röberl, Gasperl, Maierl, Steinegger and Mauskoth, or for that matter (vice versa) at the Imperial Court, no longer extant—though the blood of the former ruling family has by no means ceased to circulate in these parts.

But in the end the success of the Log Cabin Party depends largely on the same old question: Will the group of psychoanalysts from next door behave decently this time or not? Will they—as they did before midnight last year—invade the music platform, force the band to leave the platform, and proceed to perform a political satire written and produced by themselves (which nobody finds particularly funny) by way of a midnight surprise? Or, as they did two years ago, suddenly carry out the crowning of the ugliest man at the Log Cabin Party, using a crown of briar roses at that—a most uncomfortable idea!

Why can't psychoanalysts, male and female, just get drunk at a summer party like normal people? Get absolutely dead drunk like old Tataruga, for example, or quite predictably finish under the table after midnight, like the young Count Questenberg? True, in other ways that one is a bit of a freak, he wants to become an artist instead of a hunter, his interests lie with the arts rather than in the forests, but he can still knock it back with the best of his ancestors.

Ricki Tedesco has often regretted having to invite the psychoanalysts, whose sarcastic intellectual surprises disturb the unity of place and action. The basic tenets of classical drama. . . . Thus for instance the impregnation of Anna Mauskoth (unmarried) by Ferdinand Count Z. (married), at the Log Cabin Party, may be a disturbance and a tragedy, but at least it's a classical tragedy. Given a fixed place, one should be able to determine the action. Unfortunately Ricki Tedesco has let the former steward's and servants' quarters on the Tedesco property to the psychoanalyst group and the close connection, friendly landlady and tenant relationship, ties of neighbourliness and politeness, oblige her to reserve one large trestle table for the psychoanalysts. Apart from which, Ricki is undergoing analysis by the leader and uncrowned king of the group, one Dr Max Lippmann; which, as one knows, leads to a certain dependence. Consequently the ladies and gentlemen of the psychoanalyst group sit at their accustomed table again this year. Not all in dirndls or *lederhosen*, some wearing linen or summer suits, some ladies in modest evening dress: these are the intellectual rebels, who reject dirndl dress and *lederhosen* on ideological grounds. According to them the Styrian summer masquerade of Viennese lawyers, doctors, civil servants and Burgtheater actors is inadmissible blood-and-soil romanticism, albeit often, as in the case of Tataruga, it can be laid at the door of folklore fanatics of Jewish origin. Anyhow they reject all that, they will have nothing to do with folksy wish fulfilment; nevertheless, they come to Lake Grundl.

They love the scenery of the Aussee Valley just as fiercely as do the blood-and-soil romantics—the carpet of alpine flowers on the Gössler pastures, the green of Lake Grundl, the rich juiciness of the mountain meadows after a night's rain, the silhouettes of fishing punts in the early morning, on which the local trout and salmon-trout fishermen stand upright as they row past the dark silhouette of the Ressenberg, the swift-flowing water of the Traun like a keenly polished optical glass above the stones of the river-bed and glistening trout bodies, the sudden glimpses of purple Turk's head lilies amid the knee-high grass, the steel-blue stars of gentian beside the animals' drinking trough—the academic revolutionaries love it just as does the bourgeois phalanx of civil servants and court councillors. The local demi-intelligentsia—like Kniewöllner the schoolmaster and Hofer, postmaster and amateur photographer—also go in for this troubadour love-affair with the landscape and the Aussee Valley, and that is why some of the ladies and gentlemen in the psychoanalyst group are ashamed of their feelings. They therefore reject dirndl and *lederhosen*, and for this year's Log Cabin Party they have thought up a midnight surprise to dwarf all previous ones: the psychoanalysis of the late Emperor Franz Joseph in his summer villa at Bad Ischl.

On the stroke of twelve the Chinese lanterns on the terrace are extinguished, the woodmen's band sounds a flourish of trumpets (they got a special tip from the psychoanalysts for doing that), and into the half-dark ground-floor hall of the Tedesco house someone wheels a leather couch on which lies Dr Lippmann as Franz Joseph, looking absolutely genuine in hunting outfit complete with goat's beard and high nailed boots, Emperor's beard stuck on, alpenstock with azalea spray affixed on the couch beside him.

As they wheel him in Lippmann calls out in a thick voice, with eyes closed: It was very nice, it gave me great pleasure, it was very nice, it gave me great pleasure. Then the shapely psychoanalyst Lea Fischer, wearing a deliberately grandiose and grotesquely overtrimmed winter dirndl, comes to stand beside the couch and asks in a deep voice: What gave you great pleasure? Lippmann-Franz Joseph replies : Either having coffee with Frau Schratt,* or Rudolf. Lea Fischer thereupon : A decision please, Your Majesty, both together as the cause of your pleasure is a temporal impossibility. Lippmann-Franz Joseph, coughing feebly : I can't rightly say. Lea again in her deep voice : I will help you. What do you see in your mind's eye when I say Rudolf? Lippmann-Franz Joseph : The dear little whistling steamer on Lake Grundl.

Roars of laughter from the Log Cabin Party audience. The steamer which crosses Lake Grundl twice daily between Gössl and the Post Inn is, of course, called *Rudolf* —Rudolf the Emperor's son and Rudolf the steamer. Such caustic satire is levelled at the fallen. But the psychoanalysts' midnight cabaret is not the only highlight of the Log Cabin Party. The hygienic rubber goods scattered around the Tedesco park, under the hazel bushes, by the lake shore and in the boat-house—Röberl-Hans gathers them up next morning, for a consideration, with the aid of a hazel-stick bearing a pointed nail at the tip—bear witness to certain events and intrigues that I, contrary to the established teachings of the psychoanalysts' spiritual father, never dreamed of.

These are not the usual holiday perils to which pale town children are helplessly exposed : poisonous berries of deadly nightshade, landslides, torrents, poisonous mushrooms, sudden fogs, infants kidnapped by childless golden eagle couples, adder bites, fractured bones due to rash games with millstones, all these are dangers easy to size up. But how shall I ever really know whether the psychoanalytical thought-rays from the heads of Dr Lippmann and his friends and fellow-workers actually affected me?

* Katharina Schratt, a famous Burgtheater actress and Franz Joseph's mistress.

Whether they helped or harmed me? There seemed no danger of direct infection, because I was always harmlessly employed sleeping, eating, digesting, or some such childish occupation, safely isolated in the Röberls' front garden with its red and white clumps of phlox, and in bad weather I was pushed on to the veranda. All the same, something could have happened. Because my parents did more or less join in with the Lippmann group, bathed with them in the cold lake, took communal boat trips, went sailing, joined in excursions, even joined in their discussions. Thus they may have become carriers of intellectual infections, of whose underlying causes I am still unaware today.

It is simpler, however, to believe in the power of alpine spirits and to say that the Dwarf King Laurin from Bolzano or the gipsy-earring-wearing and drum-playing women of the Aussee Carnival procession protected me, from Dr Tataruga, from my trout-murdering grandmother, from the Sailor Boy in *lederhosen*—my father—and his wife in dirndl costume—my mother—from Dr Max Lippmann as the Emperor Franz Joseph, and from Ricki Tedesco, the hostess of the Log Cabin Party.

7 Garden Suburb

Even such a sheltered Nursery Self as mine will one fine day experience the horror of being uprooted. Without war or revolution or occupation by a foreign soldiery, the tragedy will come upon It, in the very midst of so-called peace.

There was a foretaste of it in the journey to the Styrian Mountains, that long rainy summer holiday in the Aussee Valley with a view of the permanently cloud-hung Dachstein Massif. But the kindly spirits of the Alps preserved It from the worst disasters. In the autumn It returned unharmed to the parental and grandparental Ringstrasse apartment, took possession again of the watchful caretaker's tomcat and the creaking *haute-bourgeois* lift, and the view from the grandparents' drawing-room of the pleasure-steamer by the Danube Canal Bridge, and the ground-hogging, white-painted steel beds of the parents. Even Sailor Boy's decision to give up that apartment in the Ringstrasse house, done up so chastely in contemporary ornament-free style by Frischherz, and to move for good next year into the Green Belt at Pötzleinsdorf, could not shatter that undamaged world which, like a great globe of milky glass, still surrounded my Nursery Self that autumn and winter.

Those unconscious hopes of a child, that uprooting is avoidable, doubtless were still with me. It took the actual move into the new house, into the new nursery, the following spring to show me that children's hopes, like the hopes of grown-ups, are as fragile as the silvered glass spheres on a Christmas tree.

The house in the garden suburb, with balcony apartment overlooking garden, as the estate agent's patter has it, is really rather pretty. From the balcony one can see the farthest spurs of the Wienerwald,* the Kahlenberg and the Leopoldsberg. The tops of six silver firs stand like guardians of a shrine about the balcony parapet of the garden apartment on the second floor, and there is fresh air in abundance. All that fresh air is what caused the move in the first place.

For unknown reasons people seem to believe that growing children need more fresh air than the full-grown, and responsible parents dare not deprive them of it. Later on the same individual will be incarcerated in ill-ventilated classrooms, dusty workshops, stuffy libraries, stinking offices and sooty factories, and then suddenly the supply of fresh air is left at the mercy of legislation. But before the pitiable Child Self is put into the ill-ventilated classroom, parents often turn into gigantic windmills whose sails shovel more and more fresh air at the tottering midget until so much fresh air positively takes away its breath (breath smelling faintly of milk, bananas and raspberry ice).

I would have got on perfectly well without this forcible feeding with fresh air. In any case Vienna is a windy city, the *urbs ventosa* of the Ancient Romans, although the maps actually call it Vindobona. Sudden gusts of wind sweeping like whip-lashes over the Ringstrasse have often slowed down the pace of May Day marches, or disarranged the black plumes of the horses drawing the black glass coach at State funerals, or driven street dust like a blizzard into the faces of conquering armies marching into the city,

* Wienerwald: Vienna Woods.

like the Germans in March 1938 or the Russians in April 1945. These Ringstrasse winds can then depart eastwards over the Danube Canal as by a wind-channel. The prevailing super-draughts of the town centre would have been quite enough fresh air for me, but the choice was not mine.

My cot was torn from its accustomed setting in the Ringstrasse apartment and tossed aboard one of those absurdly large yellow removal vans of Zdenko Dvorak & Co. In their cubist whale-bellies they accommodate not only armchairs, cupboards, beds, bedside tables and pianos, but a veritable stockpile of webbing, ropes, dust sheets, hooks, straps, and jute sacks, enough to equip a freighter bound for India. But this voyage is only from the Schottenring, past the Stock Exchange to the Schotten Gate, westwards through Währinger Strasse, past the Confectioner's Gothic of the Votive Church, meets the Outer Ring at the Comic Opera, changes gear and elopes with my cot via Gersthof to Pötzleinsdorf, to the already familiar garden-overlooking balcony apartment. These removal robbers—in my father's pay, mark you—tear my little cot out of the whale-belly, carry it through a wrought-iron gate, up two storeys, put it in a room with a view of the side of a house covered with creeper, and vanish—bailiffs of deracination.

Furniture, and especially children's beds, could certainly be considered uprooted from their environment like young trees and tender plants. But these muscle-men don't go in for such sensitive fancies. I have to get my bearings in this new situation as best I can. Register the view of creeper-covered wall, this ivylike wall plant changes colour like a chameleon: green, yellow, red, according to the time of year, natural enough in an outdoor plant, but the

Nursery Self assumes that it is the wall itself which changes colour.

The pane of fluted frosted glass in the door, which fragments light coming from the hall so that figures beyond it appear to move like characters in a shadow play, is another strange novelty, as is the second door in the nursery—a double door to the parents' bedroom: the space between is dark and mysterious. The second door might be locked. Then while one is in the dark bit between the two doors, someone might turn the key in the first door too, and then one would be trapped in the divide between child's room and parents' bedroom.

Not that my blurred Nursery Self yet laboured under the curse of apprehending such unambiguous terrors.

Surely there must have been more to the Pötzleinsdorfer balcony apartment than colour-changing, creeper-covered outside walls and the dark space between parents' bedroom and nursery. How, for instance, were the Frischherz apartment effects distributed in the living-room with the balcony? What sinister items of furniture infest the large, newly furnished room beside the living-room? What is the maid's room like? Have kitchen and bathroom been relegated to the rank of second violins, fiddling away mechanically in the balcony flat symphony?

Two corner-stones of the Frischherz interior master plan based on the no-ornament theory of aesthetics—the white-silk shaded lamp with the two brass rings and the rose-hip knob, and the white-projected but owing to Sailor Boy's objection brown-executed, dining-table—have been demoted from their central intellectual significance by a new acquisition. In place of the Frischherz bookshelves, Sailor Boy has had a hip-high bookcase made, going the whole length of the room, but not according to Frischherz specifications. Sailor Boy's collection of first editions has grown by the metre, and my Nursery Self edges past this intellectual wall, towering far above Its childish head, when It wants to go out on the balcony. There is one shelf attractive beyond all others: pretty little volumes, just hand-sized, with pigskin spines bearing red labels with gold lettering: today I know them to be Goethe's *Collected Works*, last authorised edition during the poet's lifetime.

On the way to the balcony that time the full charm is lost in the great mass of red labels imprinted with letters of gold. I stop, turn to the *Collected Works of Goethe*, authorised edition, and with both hands shove the pretty, hand-high volumes into the depths of the bookcase, like so many toy bricks. Sailor Boy, who is sitting under the lamp with the red rose-hip knob, reading the paper like a proper father, thereupon leaps to his feet, advances menacingly upon my Nursery Self and pulls Its arms away from the bookcase, before the remaining *Works*, as also the *Posthumous Works* and the rare *Index Volume* of Goethe's *Collected Works*, authorised edition, can be shoved like bricks in a child's building set into the depths of the bookcase. You mustn't do that, says Sailor Boy, reinforcing this Thou Shalt Not with a ritual slap on the back of my right hand. For my part, I did not forgive Sailor Boy this Mosaic laying down of the law, this first corporal punishment, until many years later, when I discovered the value of Goethe's *Collected Works*, authorised edition, set out in an antiquarian's catalogue. One can get to the balcony without stopping at Goethe's *Collected Works*, authorised edition. The balcony, with its view of the Kahlenberg—the Polish King Sobieski came down from the Kahlenberg with the relief army in 1683, drove away the Turks, those rascally Muslims, saved Vienna from the Crescent, saved it for the Holy Roman Empire of the German nation and for the Christian Occident. Fortunately the child's view does not have to go that far back into history; the school, which will set it to that hard labour one day, has no jurisdiction as yet. How, then, does the Nursery Self occupy Itself in Its balcony setting? It looks at what is nearest, the balcony of the apartment below. There sits the retired Leopold Ritter von Wipperer-Stroheim, a former director of the Danube Steamship Navigation Company, that limited liability company linking the Danube nations. In front of a small smoking-table on which there is always a glass of water, he sits reading in his grandfather chair (whose carved feet are fitted with castors). In the morning, if it's fine, the castors run with their armchair burden on to the balcony, and in the evening they run back into the living-room. The grandfather chair belonging to the retired knight, Leopold von Wipperer-Stroheim, is not, in fact, a *perpetuum mobile*, as the Nursery Self thinks (castors not being visible from above). Nor is Sir Leopold himself a *perpetuum mobile*, though he may appear to be, from the way he spends his days.

Weather permitting, he sits with his book on his armchair on the balcony, and without benefit of knife and fork he, so to speak, devours page after page of the book, like goulash. He smacks his lips over the delicious intellectual sustenance, an intellectual lip-smacking, the joy of it, pausing comfortably now and then to take a sip of water from the glass on the smoking-table; all of which is explained by the bland and eminently digestible quality of the said intellectual sustenance. Sir Leopold has preserved from his school days, through the intervening period of active service to the day when my Nursery Self first sights his white hair, the capacity of feeling the utmost excitement in reading the adventures of Winnetou the Warrior, following the flight of Maya the Bee* with passionate interest, and deriving far more pleasure from Jack London's wildest tales than from the *Divine Comedy*, the *Sorrows of Werther*, or the fate of the Buddenbrooks. Thus he is a sort of *perpetuum mobile* after all, though not in any technical sense: a *perpetuum mobile* of the adolescent lust for adventure, as yet unmodified by real life. It is amazing how he has preserved that through all his active life with the Danube Steamship Navigation Company and into his retirement. . . .

Can it be that the Danube Steamship Navigation Company gave him no outlet for his adventurous longings? I find that hard to credit, remembering how the Imperial and High Court Advocate, Sailor Boy's father, used to stand on the balcony of his Ringstrasse apartment, looking down at the Danube Canal and daydreaming.

I could buy a ticket, first or second class, from the Danube Steamship Navigation Company, go on board and, smoking Virginia cigars, listen to the lapping of the waves, past the Thebener Gate, Pressburg, past Budapest, Belgrade, past flying cormorants and dancing peasants in Romanian national dress, go down as far as the Black Sea —I could do all that.

And an immense adventure it would have seemed to the High Court Advocate.

Leopold von Wipperer-Stroheim could have had this adventure at no cost whatsoever; being a director of the Danube Steamship Navigation Company he was conveyed gratis. But adventures at the company's expense cannot satisfy the truly adventurous spirit. An adventure grows

* Popular animal book for juveniles, by Waldeman Bonsels, comparable to *Tarka the Otter*.

with the price one has to pay for it, the highest price being one's own life; so the most splendid adventure must always involve risking one's life. Sir Leopold to his grief reached the age and state of retirement in perfect health and completely undamaged (during his term of office he never once got into a situation where his life was at risk).

What a pair they make—Leopold the retired knight, aware that in his whole life he never risked his neck, and my Nursery Self, as yet unaware that throughout life, that relentless, single-track process of growing up, one is constantly in mortal danger.

I won't say any more about my parents just now, about their life in the beautiful new apartment in the Green Belt, having already reported on their lives in the Ringstrasse apartment and at the *Neue* and *Neueste Stern*, not to mention their summer life with the Noble Savages in the mountains of Styria. Someone might think I was out for revenge by exposing them—even in this fresh garden suburb air, than which nothing could be more conducive to calm and healthy respiration—yet again. Also Sailor Boy could reproach me (justly) that I was only returning to him and his wife yet again, and not for the last time either, because I could find nothing to say about Bruno Wimmer, the owner of the house.

Every evening at 6 on the dot Bruno Wimmer (the child staring down at the garden from the balcony is unaware that he runs a bookshop in town and is indeed Sailor Boy's business partner) appears in that selfsame garden, sits down on the white-painted, immaculately clean garden bench, which stands under one of the fir trees whose tops reach the balcony, takes a silver cigarette case from his jacket pocket, snaps it open with the practised one-handed gesture of a heavy smoker, fishes out a cigarette and taps it against the lid of the case before wedging it in the mouth of his well-tanned sportsman's face and lighting it. This chore passes the time until Frau Wimmer, that notably good and thrifty housekeeper, comes into the garden. Did she not insist in the friendliest way when they moved in that Sailor Boy's wife must take a look at her household accounts? Was she not trying to show the younger woman—via the contemplation of painstakingly kept entries for onions, chives, veal, beef and pork, matches too, and shoe-polish, stain removers and greaseproof paper—a vision of the modest, frugal yet contented life? Far away from that Ringstrasse world where married women, mothers of children, are actually said to have love-affairs, and where members of great and ancient families think nothing of making advances to unbaptised ladies, provided they are beautiful, and responsive in the right way.

Frau Wimmer comes into the garden, a fair day's pay for a fair day's work, sets the silver tray with snow-white tray-cloth, embroidered initials J.W., Josephine Wimmer, and on it coffee, a sugary bun and a glass of water, ice-cold water in a frost-misted glass, down in front of Bruno Wimmer.

Now they drink coffee together and know themselves to be well off, because they do things sensibly. Many are not so well off, because they don't have such a careful wife, don't keep accounts, drink wine and champagne instead of coffee adulterated with chicory or water which has been chilled to the temperature of spring-water by being allowed to run. Many are outwardly better off—industrialists, famous advocates, successful artists, foreigners, gamblers and Jews (sound on the surface, and rotten within)—but we, Bruno and Josephine Wimmer tell themselves, are not among the better off or the worse off. But our loneliness—they don't say that, but a pastor, a bishop, a spiritual adviser, the Cardinal Archbishop of Vienna, might have been able to tell them all the same—needs to be assuaged, resolved, brought to a happy ending.

We can expect nothing from the Schmölzers, who run after every glimpse of a red flag, except spiky nests on communal fortress towers, where they will raise broods of machine-guns in place of swallows; the Tedescos and Tatarugas, who run after stocks and shares, have nothing but ridicule for us. Our kingdom for a pro-Wimmer policy! But we've been a Republic for too long, we have no kingdom left to give. Who will give our son Wilhelm, Wilhelm Theodor Wimmer as it says on his baptismal certificate, faith in the future? The gaping child staring down at the garden from the balcony sees only coffee drinkers' and smokers' gestures, the muscular mechanics essential to the consumption of buns. How could It know that a faith in the future was needed as well?

Certainly this faith in the future, within this multifamily villa in Pötzleinsdorf, is demanded most fiercely and desperately and frequently by Bruno and Josephine Wimmer, but not usually in public: it is a secret longing, a desire concealed in their breast, like unrequited love—which everyone assumes to exist in Josephine Wimmer's mousy sister, Fräulein Emmy. She nurses and looks after her and Josephine's mother, most devotedly, although—or perhaps because?—Emmy's share of the house has not yet passed from her mother's possession (unlike her married sister's share). Why Fräulein Emmy should have to put up with everyone's roguish, untested and never actually uttered (only that mocking twist of the mouth on the part of whoever is looking at her gives it away) conviction that this mousy Fräulein Emmy harbours, must harbour, such unrequited longing for love, is beyond me.

Let me ask frankly, is it not at least possible that Fräulein Emmy feels quite content on Sundays when she goes to the parish church of St Laurence and St Gertrude, and then—her mother's state of health permitting—walks through the Pötzleinsdorf Schloss Park, where the nineteenth-century sandstone statues of Flora and Fortuna, twice larger than life, stand at either side offering their message to posterity.

Castle built by Baron Geymüller—champagne parties, fireworks, closed carriages, actresses brought from town in the middle of the night, Pavilion of Love with Stone of Friendship in a concealed hollow in the English-style Park, double staircase in the garden with a grand sweep, ascend one side, descend the other, singing, laughing, music-making stone cherubs in a circle—all gambled away, all wasted : Ashes to ashes. . . .

Fräulein Emmy, rightly feeling all this has nothing to do with her, may however on occasion stop at the wayside shrine on the Gersthofer Strasse, showing Madonna and Holy Trinity, and an inscription dating from 1776 :

> WHEN THE TURK CAME INTO THE LAND IN THE YEAR 1683 ALL IMAGES OF GOD WERE DESTROYED. BUT THESE STAYED QUITE UNHARMED 16 ANNO 87.

Then, without exuding any spinsterish excess of piety or suppressing any unrequited desires, she returns to her business of caring for her mother and dressmaking (Fräulein Emmy is a skilled dressmaker). I could even imagine that the burning desire for a faith in the future, so strong in her sister Josephine Wimmer and her brother-in-law

Bruno Wimmer, was not present in Fräulein Emmy, consanguinity notwithstanding.

Nor do the hopes of the housekeeper Maria Jellinek regarding her future quite match those of the Wimmers. Despite the strained national economy, Herr Jellinek is not yet out of work, he has not yet lost his job as a builder's foreman, although his boss mutters vague threats when things come to a standstill because too many men don't turn up on a Monday and Jellinek can only shrug his shoulders helplessly. I'm no prison warder, sir, says Jellinek. Stop mucking about, Jellinek, the boss replies. All the same, Jellinek might lose his job, and so, shortly after we have moved in, Maria Jellinek accepts the Sailor Boy's wife's suggestion that she should cook for us, for a small consideration, working only half-days that is. At intervals she has to keep going downstairs to see to her housekeeper's flat. Deposit a nicely crisped Schnitzel, a plate of cucumber salad, a piece of apple-strudel or three to six apricot dumplings, put them by, keep them for Herr Jellinek's homecoming in the evening. Crumbs, to put it scripturally, that fall from the rich man's table, although what falls is in fact Schnitzel, cucumber salad, apple-strudel and apricot dumplings. Apart from this, she gets paid by all the tenants for cleaning the house, so that the monthly income of the Jellineks stems from three separate sources, but Maria Jellinek would be glad if at least one of these could yield a bit more.

The journey to Böhmisch-Leipa, says Maria Jellinek in her German tinged with the accents of her mother tongue, to see my brothers and sisters, I can barely afford it once a year. Maria Jellinek's faith in the future means hoping to find herself one day in the position where, without having to give it much thought, without having to pinch and scrape, without having to drop meat from the menu or wait for the crumbs from the rich man's table, she may even be able to take a taxi, so that she doesn't have to lug those two heavy bags full of presents (in her mind's eye she can just see them bursting apart at the seams) to the tram stop, and have that taxi drive her to the North Western Station, and buy herself a return ticket to Böhmisch-Leipa, just like that.

In this system of co-ordinates, between Jellinek and Wimmer, Ritter von Wipperer-Stroheim and Fräulein Emmy, is there nothing colourful and gay, that can sing and laugh and be of some use to a child, with which one can play and rush about and have fun? Something like a parrot which can fluff out its feathers and jabber away after you, 'Good morning', 'Good morning, ducky'—or like a paper kite, its tail weighted with bundles of grass, climbing carefree on its string into the sky and, nodding in the wind, smiling down with a good-natured paper kite smile? Simply something to play with—a child of the same age would be best of all. But there is no such thing in this multifamily villa full of grown-ups.

The only *homo ludens* round here, wealthy Camillo Gutmann, born in Prague (he brought Sailor Boy capital to acquire a new business and became a sleeping partner in it, this was after Sailor Boy had parted company with Bruno Wimmer, amid lengthy negotiations and without a cash settlement: Wimmer kept the old business premises and said to Sailor Boy, I'm afraid I can only pay you half your share at the moment, my assets are tied up), this Camillo Gutmann gets the best corner room in our new apartment for a *pied à terre*, but he only uses it occasionally and mostly doesn't get home until midnight when he is in Vienna. In this whole house he is the one with whom

I get on best. Camillo Gutmann has the same playful attitude to life as any Nursery Self.

Intact financial status (on the father's side—the Gutmann Bank in Prague stayed solvent even after that Black Monday on Wall Street) facilitates that, as do certain estates and a medieval house with pointed arches, 'Zum Himmel', in Salzburg, plus the inn and hotel complex bearing the same name (all this on the mother's side). A carefree time at grammar school, broken off just before the decisive final examinations; on the other hand, nannies and tutors transmitted to him a precognitive facility in Czech, French and English (so that multilinguistic *jeux d'esprit* trip off his tongue as charmingly and effortlessly as a ballroom conversation between waltz and gallopade). Hardly a man of letters, but a man of the world, who was already full of delicious memories of youthful dalliance in the famous Prague establishment 'Gogo' at No. 6 Gemsengasse, when I first consciously knew him.

Prague's 'Gogo' offers the same or similar attractions as Madame Rosa's salon in Vienna, but the very name 'Gogo' sounds so much more playful. Do you feel like 'Gogo' tonight? Shall we go to 'Gogo's'? They have marvellous food there, too, you can drink champagne, the writer Werfel may be at the piano, and you get Verdi arias from Piccaver thrown in—for nothing, and much better sung than at the Opera, because he's in a much better mood at 'Gogo's'. Moreover, you can leave the Salon Goldschmied (its officially registered name) again, over the flags of the tiled hall, without having indulged in any 'Gogo' under those fine plasterwork ceilings: the white tiles are patterned with grapes—O Bacchus, O Gogo!

Camillo Gutmann is delighted when the Prague friends of his youth call him 'Gogo' Gutmann. But Salons Rosa and Goldschmied alike are not, *fortunately* as my great-grandfather Solomon from the Moravian ghetto would say (had he even known of the existence of these grand bourgeois abysses of Vienna and Prague—he who joined his forefathers pure in spirit), even in our emancipated age, playgrounds for a growing Nursery Self.

It may well have been 'Gogo's' that helped to make Camillo Gutmann completely and fundamentally different from what otherwise surrounded me in the multifamily villa amidst all that fresh air from the Wienerwald: the three Wimmers, the two Wipperer-Stroheims, Fräulein Emmy and her mother, Herr and Frau Jellinek, and my own family helped to make him the nowadays wrongfully neglected and all but forgotten ideal of *homo ludens*, living every moment unreservedly to the full.

Who but 'Gogo' Gutmann, for example, was prepared, when leaving the house in the morning, to doff overcoat and briefcase again and keep the taxi waiting half an hour in front of the house, in order to play the mouth-organ with me, a Nursery Self of the utmost commercial insignificance? Who but 'Gogo' Gutmann ever crawled through the garden with me, he being in his dinner-jacket and on the way to the Opera, looking for a lost Indian head-dress? He thereby missed the first act of *Traviata*, and the head-dress wasn't found until the next day after all, in Frau Jellinek's dustbin in the cellar. Who but 'Gogo' Gutmann—this story has nothing to do with me, but is characteristic—on an important business trip to the Leipzig Book Fair would have got out of the train prematurely at Znaim instead? As the train approaches the cucumber town of Znaim, 'Gogo' sees dozens of marvellous red fire-engines decorated with garlands driving at walking pace through the streets of this South Moravian town, accompanied by brass bands. Gogo asks the ticket collector what all this means. Centenary celebrations of the Voluntary Fire Service, says the ticket collector, inauguration of the hose, firemen's band, illuminations. Whereupon Gogo gets off and spends two days in Znaim, although he is not a fireman, and has neither friends nor relatives in Znaim. Now that is living up to one's ideals, not to let business deals get you down, dates at the Leipzig Book Fair, where clerks enter at the exact minute predetermined days in advance, not to be dominated by the whole minute-hand world of monthly settlements. The world that worships the loose-leaf calendar, offering it sacrifices (as to a golden calf) of cash books, staplers, typewriter ribbons and order books with carbon copy sheets, erasers with small brushes attached, stamping pads, paper scissors, inkwells, blotting paper, revolting little red sponges with which the cashier moistens her finger-stall before counting the money. Never knuckle under to this paper world breeding paper money.

Whenever business deals look particularly promising, the crucial dates are at hand and the clerks nervously fidgeting outside the boss's office, Gogo will tend to pause and say to himself: If you do not become as little children, the minute hand will leap out of the office clock, change into a hypodermic syringe, inject lethal business air into the veins of the most successful salesman, the clerk will sew epaulettes to the shoulders of his black office suit and with his customary punctuality carry out something horrifying, the date of completion will complete one's own fate, ineluctable as death itself.

So ludicrous a posthumous demonification of things, Gogo Gutmann simply dismissed out of hand. No *homo ludens* should draw speculative cube roots out of everyday things. Nor had Gogo Gutmann the slightest intention of doing so.

He was always getting fresh ideas; only a free and gamesome spirit like his could have thought up something like the children's loo in Sailor Boy's bookshop. Even Gogo Gutmann has a residue of the bourgeois businessman's and banker's pride; at least, they tried to talk him into having it. First his mother, Stephanie Gutmann, *née* Stössel of Salzburg, was on at him about it, and then, repeatedly and very forcefully, his respectable brother Mario. You must take some interest in your invested capital, says Mario, examine the books, keep an eye on your partner (that's Sailor Boy). Gogo prefers most things to going through the books, the pages of those account books exhale unutterable tedium, whether decorated with figures or as yet mere headed blanks—a *homo ludens* like Gogo Gutmann could only enjoy himself here by swapping around sums from debit to credit side, then investing the sum total in the first Austrian Class Lottery, and awaiting the big win in the Salon Goldschmied, No. 6 Gemsengasse, Prague.

But even Gogo is not wholly consistent, even he acts out of character at times, wishing to prove himself to Stephanie Gutmann, *née* Stössel of Salzburg, and to his respectable brother Mario. He therefore uses the holiday period or times when Sailor Boy is away on business to make independent dispositions in the great town bookshop with adjoining publishing house (near the Graben, behind the Plague Monument), place spontaneous book orders, deal with unknown authors, and above all—he does want his partner to see some trace of his Big Chief game on his return—make minor innovations like, for instance, the children's loo, which had not been previously discussed with Sailor Boy.

Of course the installation of the children's loo was a source of peculiar satisfaction to me, since the Punch and

Judy shows in the Children's Books Department involved such unusual excitement. The puppeteer, who was condemned—especially during the Christmas period—to non-stop Punch and Judy performances by order of Sailor Boy, was not content to produce only the usual scenes and tricks : Hallo, children! All together now: Hallo, Mr Punch! Louder, I can't hear you—that's better : Hallo, Mr Punch! Where's the policeman, children, behind you, Punch, behind you, thump, bash the policeman on the head—no, this puppeteer hired by Sailor Boy to enliven the children's books turnover had retained his artistic pride despite the Depression.

His puppet theatre could produce thunder and lightning, rocks opened and behind them flickered the red glow of some infernal abyss, fairies locked up in mountains begged with squeaky voices to be set free and were then whisked in Icarus flights from their rock prison over the stage to freedom. There I sat in the darkened Children's Books Department and in great excitement we watched these fairy flights to freedom, accompanied by bursts of thunder. All this stage thunder, these fairy flights, though they're just to promote the Christmas book trade, have their effect on the psychosomatic balance of the Nursery Self.

It's easy to talk, now. Every reasonably competent academic can rationalise his physical urges—be they urinary or genital—into a humanistically trimmed system, which divides cause from effect as much as possible, depositing these weighty concepts in widely separated chambers of the mental household. But for me in those days it was a great satisfaction and relief when my nanny's sure grip swiftly removed me from the diuretic fairy world of thunder and lightning, to the children's loo—only half the height of a grown-up loo, even pre-school age children could mount it without effort. The other children, strangers to me, must have felt the same; from our point of view, Gogo's independent innovation was a wonderful thing.

True, Sailor Boy on his return beat his fist furiously upon the wooden lid of the new acquisition and forbade Gogo to set foot on the premises until further notice. But even today, looking back, I find myself taking Gogo's part. The generation gap is not, after all, bridged by my realisation that I am now exactly the same age Sailor Boy was when he denied Gogo any more say in the business until further notice, or because I no longer need a children's loo when a fairy imprisoned in a rock begs me to free her. I still feel closer to the Party of the Absurd than to any of the other parties that canvass my vote.

Despite Punch and Judy shows and jolly games with Uncle Gogo, though my paternal grandmother came from the Schottenring apartment to the well-aired garden suburb, bringing me sweets, or a Red Indian outfit with feathered head-dress, a Chinese lantern or something else, though my maternal grandfather came from the *Neueste Stern* in the East via the Outer Ring and the Währingerstrasse—basically it was a lonely life, without siblings or playmates of the same age. In the multifamily villa there were, as already mentioned, no children at all. The neighbouring houses had no children either. Perhaps all those quantities of fresh air drove the children away. Or perhaps people lost the urge to procreate, what with civil war and the Depression. Perhaps the very name 'Century of the Child' points to a shortage of children, the goods in short supply becoming a wishful symbol? Dubious phenomena always have been made acceptable by conferring pretentious names upon them : a hero's death, patriotism, martyr, official secret, *lèse-majesté*, a foeman worthy of one's steel, trustee savings stock.

Anyhow, Sailor Boy's wife must have noticed the lack at some stage. A playmate was co-opted. Why Gusti Wawra of all people was chosen, I don't know. I think the housekeeper Maria Jellinek had something to do with it. She knew all about the age, class and religious set-up of all the multifamily, two-family or single-family villas within the area of Schafberg, Pötzleinsdorfer Strasse and right up to the wrought-iron gate with the two stone lions at the entrance to the Pötzleinsdorfer Schloss Park. The Secret Police know what they're doing when, in suspicious circumstances, they always question the caretakers first. Evidently, then, my mother in her desperate search for a playmate for me appealed to this extensive knowledge of Frau Jellinek's regarding the age, class and religious structure of the houses in the triangle demarcated by Schafberg, Schloss Park and Pötzleinsdorfer Strasse, for it was on the hand of Frau Jellinek that Gusti Wawra appeared at our first play session, but he was immediately, before even entering the nursery, taken over by my nanny—washed, nose blown, clothes changed, combed. (So here is Gusti Wawra ready and passed for companionship.) This is what happens when decisions of vital importance to a lonely child are left to a good-natured but not very far-sighted housekeeper. She produces a dirty, ragged Gusti Wawra, one of five children of a scene-shifter at the Comic Opera who is, however, usually out of work. Gusti's mother is the housekeeper of a Schönbrunn-yellow, single-family villa—hence the damp basement flat for five children and the mostly unemployed scene-shifter. A child of the gutter, so to speak. Frau Jellinek says with a kindly smile in her Bohemian lilt: Play nicely together, Gusti and you.

I was very happy to have someone to play with. And we were certainly a good match in age, but classwise—a blunder on the part of Frau Jellinek. And what about the religious aspect? Can my Protestant and Jewish ancestors have anything in common with Gusti's Roman Catholic ones? But a Nursery Self of pre-school age hasn't the faintest idea of such theological difficulties of later life, and very sensibly keeps off the Class War too, though perhaps I owed some degree of involvement to my grandfather at the *Neueste Stern*. Nor has It, thank God, even the vaguest conception of the actual Holy Trinity in our latitudes, consisting (except in Roman Catholic religious instruction) not of Father, Son and Holy Ghost, but of Jewish, Catholic and Protestant angles to the triangle. All the angles together don't, however, result in a beautiful geometric God figure in the shape of a triangle as drawn on the board by the father-instructor—quite the contrary. . . .

I had no intention of starting either a class war or a religious war with Gusti Wawra. Gusti and I decided to organise some Red Indian wars, not against each other of course. Naturally we both belonged to the same Red Indian tribe, which pitched its tents in the farthest corner of the garden, the only really wild bit, overgrown with shrubs, in this otherwise well-gravelled villa garden. Each family has a corner of the garden to itself. Every spring each family puts garden table and garden chairs into its corner, these get freshly painted every spring and in autumn are carried back into the cellar, where they hibernate. Only one corner is without gravel and without table and chairs. Frau Jellinek sweeps dead leaves into this corner, throws dry twigs on the heap, keeps gravel rake and spade in this corner. Here, too, an Indian tribe consisting only of Gusti Wawra and myself can find refuge. In the morning my nanny helps us to put on our Red Indian outfits, to arrange our savage head-dresses composed of dyed chicken feathers. My grandmother gave Gusti Wawra a complete Indian outfit too, no different in detail from mine: same head-dress, same material for leggings and jacket, same number of tomahawks and bowie-knives of silvery papier mâché. Gusti Wawra must not be at any disadvantage while playing with me.

Why Wawra senior, the scene-shifter, thought so little of this honest effort at class justice on the part of Sailor Boy and his wife, I cannot now guess. Perhaps he never found out that his son Gusti gets the most delicious elevenses from Nanny, as I do—ham sandwiches, bananas and milk chocolate—as we sit in the tent behind Frau Jellinek's leaf-mould and compost heap, waiting for the enemy, papier mâché tomahawks on our knees, chewing bananas and milk chocolate. Unfortunately no enemy tribe ever turns up. That's because there are too few children on the war-path in the Pötzleinsdorf garden suburb. It might have been feasible to import children from farther away, from Neuwaldegg, Grinzing, Hernals and Ottakring, put them into Indian outfits and set them attacking the tent in which Gusti Wawra and I sat—it would have made us happy and given meaning and purpose to our Indian existence behind the Jellinek compost heap. Nothing like that happened. Nobody procured any enemies for us. Perhaps the children of Neuwaldegg and Grinzing, let alone the working-class children of Hernals and Ottakring, had less attentive nannies and were not stuffed with ham rolls, bananas and chocolate like Gusti and I were, so they might not have been strong enough to survive the long approach march with aggressive spirits undimmed. Anyhow, we decided to give up Indian life after many uneventful mornings of waiting—in the afternoons one has to sleep, and afterwards it's too dark to sit in a tent—and to spend our playtime in ways less dependent on natural phenomena.

I suggested trying to make our living as street musicians, and Gusti Wawra agreed. We decided to start in a modest way. A mouth-organ and two receptacles for money, one an old felt hat, the other a money box of silvered tin—such was our equipment. We took up our position in front of my nursery door. I played the mouth-organ and Gusti rattled the tin and pointed his foot at the felt hat which lay upturned on the floor. Then Gusti played the mouth-organ and I looked after the money. We made a good team, we were successful. Frau Jellinek threw ten groschen into the hat, Nanny gave us a donation, Gogo Gutmann gave us something, Sailor Boy and his wife supported us, we no longer had to wait for alien Indians that never turned up. And it all took place in the apartment, which was advantageous in the cold season. My nanny was well content.

But when Gusti said now we ought to try being musicians, complete with mouth-organ, felt hat and silver tin, at his home for a change, my nanny began to make excuses, would not allow it—but Sailor Boy's wife said, Yes, do play together at Gusti's house too. So one day we did sit on the splintery softwood floor of the scene-shifter's musty basement, rattled the silvered tin box and held out the hat. I was surprised by the Wawra children's lack of interest; I was surprised, too, that the younger ones wore no pants. The smell of the basement, a mixture of stagnant air, damp washing, boiled cabbage and infant Wawras, positively amazed me. I blew on the mouth-organ and looked around me wide-eyed.

It is easy to see I was prepared neither for the Class War nor for the Class Peace. I was not even prepared for war and peace of a more general kind, although human beings always find themselves in one state or the other. I didn't even know what war and peace were. Are all children really so unprepared for the most prevalent circumstances? On the other hand, do the others, the adult inhabitants of the villas between the Schafberg, Pötzleinsdorfer Strasse and the stone lions by the wrought-iron gate to the Pötzleinsdorf Schloss Park, know any more about it? They who bear the wonderful distinctions and caste marks of the human race which are denied to children—soprano-high or bass-deep voices, false plaits and genuine beards, axillary hair and pubic hair, legal and illegal party cards, weapons licensed or unlicensed, varnished or bitten fingernails, convictions firm as rock, truss belts, tail coats with medals and evening-dresses, false teeth, bank accounts, patriotic pride, honorary titles, flat chests and swelling, starched shirt-fronts, cirrhotic livers, souls receptive to Beauty and Truth, nostalgia, local sentiment, an undeclared bankruptcy. These people, so deeply experienced in living, do they know how long the peace will last, when war will come, from where it will come, what will cause it? We are a small peaceful country, they whisper at afternoon teas, evening parties, musical evenings—but things are not going well for us.

Even in Ricki Tedesco's town salon (Ricki doesn't only keep open house in summer beside Lake Grundl: her Viennese salon of music, literature and politics in the art-nouveau villa at the edge of the Wienerwald is almost as famous as Old Tedesco, her grandfather, was in his star role of Wallenstein in the Hofburg Theatre of Old Prohaska—the Bureaucrat Emperor, cockatoo plume, pen-wiper and well-chewed quill, the post of Master of the Imperial Household carries responsibility for the Fine Arts), even in this intellectually alert, politically semi-alert salon, the guests whisper to one another: How long can things stay peaceful, when danger threatens, if it does, from where will it come, why, is there any danger at all, any immediate danger, for what reason, why?—we are a small and peaceful country, but things are not too good. Just how bad are things?

Looking around Ricki Tedesco's salon, one's glance falls on a marble sideboard with art-nouveau ornamentation, stylised lilies bending towards one another, above it a flight of wild geese of mother-of-pearl inlay in the ebony-black wall panelling—wild geese vanishing in an imaginary winter sky, a Chinese scene really, a poem by Li Tai-po or Tu Fu in mother of pearl and ebony black, a dream vessel really, and why not? Is that worth mentioning? Is beautifully curved art-nouveau ornamentation in a grand bourgeois Pötzleinsdorf villa—according to the land register, the Tedesco villa is in fact situated in Döbling, but we needn't be too pedantic about boundaries—anything out of the ordinary?

A slow flight of wild geese in mother of pearl, in troubled times, surely that can soothe a mind distressed by the Spanish Civil War or the military potential of Lance-Corporal A. H., who was badly burned by a lewisite combination gas in 1918? Flights of wild geese, trains of thought, the poet-Emperor of China sits in his war-tent watching the first snow-flakes settling in the black manes of the short-legged sturdy Kirgiz horses, gives an order before breakfast that two dozen insubordinate officials in the neighbouring province are to be beheaded, after breakfast watches the wild geese flying south and thinks of his distant beloved, and has them bring him black ink and a brush and draws a calligraphic poem about wild geese flying south, on

Imperial rice paper, which he then sends by Imperial messenger (who also carries the above-mentioned decapitation order in his saddle-bag) to his distant beloved—far off days, better days. . . ?

Are these the thoughts of Monsieur Aristide Lapiné, banker, currency specialist, spare-time translator of German poetry into French, guest of honour this evening in Ricki Tedesco's salon? As he stands motionless in his tail coat in front of the marble sideboard and, instead of looking at poached eggs, red lobster claws, Russian salad, pistachio cream and *crème à la vanille*, bottles of champagne, white wine and red wine, lets his eyes follow the mother-of-pearl wild geese, his thoughts roam free. What does the Emperor of China know about the course of events in alpine Austria after the Depression, after the forcible silencing of noisy socialists of the *Neue* and *Neueste Stern*? Schölzer has done time in the detention camp for political subversives; the Neighbour squatted beside him on the same prison mattress, having been kicked out of Parliament; they partook in unison of the same watery prison cabbage soup. Thus the old comrades were reunited, embraced and said Friendship, and at last they had time to talk again about the early days of the Movement. Do you remember when we sold the last brick for the building of the *Neue Stern*, what a party that was! Here on Holy Days they spooned up burnt potatoes, and on Sundays, burnt rice pudding, from the same tin bowl, all served to them by their honourable political opponents. 'For what you receive may the Lord make you truly thankful', and 'For ever and ever amen', if they were not actually, at the hour of their political—and for some, indeed, physical—death, forcibly offered Holy Communion, that eternally satisfying solace of the Faith which is the true source of happiness, save that they got it against all their free-thinking volition. The same honourable political opponents now look for salvation, not like the lilies of the field to the Lord above, but to Monsieur Aristide Lapiné, who has come to Vienna in the service of the French State to negotiate the loan which is the only true source of happiness, and perhaps something else as well (a mutual aid treaty, military aid, arms deliveries, what doesn't one hope for, long for . . .)?

But what does the Emperor of China know about events in post-Depression alpine Austria? Ricki Tedesco's salon is really more of an artistic, musical and literary salon, perhaps the foremost around here, as she likes to say in jest.

'My dear Aristide Lapiné,' says Ricki, taking his arm, 'forget the bank rate for tonight and live with us in that generous style which is a necessary prerequisite for the flowering and appreciation of the Fine Arts.' Then, turning to her guests: 'We welcome Monsieur Lapiné as the finest translator of Goethe's poems into the language of Racine, Pascal and Voltaire.' Clapping, murmurs of assent; Aristide Lapiné allows Ricki to load his plate with poached eggs, and selects a light Vöslauer wine. Now he can throw off the banker and put on the Goethe translator instead, he gets introduced in all directions.

Dr Lippmann and his associates, the psychoanalyst group of Ricki's Log Cabin Party by Lake Grundl, do not appear at the art-nouveau salon in town. They all seem to be involved in obscure political intrigues. One can only help them, as Ricki Tedesco does for old friendship's sake, by keeping absolutely quiet about their very existence. Like Ricki Tedesco, one leaves them completely alone in their illegal way of life, not only this evening but all the time. In any case, they would have ruined the atmosphere, who knows but they might have demanded that Schönberg's *Verklärte Nacht* be laid on instead of Schubert's Trout Quintet. They would have shattered the prevailing muted optimism by vouchsafing confidences about their comrades in exile in Brünn and elsewhere; in short, they would have made leftist mischief, and they might even have interrupted Alexander Monti, the famous impresario, when, on the way to the music-room, he says to Monsieur Lapiné: 'Welcome to our alpine country, as our trusted friend and as the friend of the League of Nations, who will defend a small nation's desire to remain free with the aid of the Great Powers. . . . Tonight we hope you will enjoy with us the music and the wine of this country between North and South. Your health!'

Monti raises his glass, Lapiné nods amiably, and both take a good swig at the delicate Vöslauer. Side by side they continue, crossing the border between drawing-room and music-room, past the great glazed double doors. The theme of wild geese is carried on in the glass of the doors: transparent wild geese in this case, illuminated from both rooms, a double magic lantern effect—fly, birds, fly!

Lapiné and Monti sit down in the front seats in the music-room, pledge each other once more, look about them and realise that the chamber music is not going to start as soon as all that. The other guests drift in very slowly, stand about in groups, talking, bunches of drawing-room grapes pressing the juice out of one another: how long can the peace last, if danger there be, from where does it threaten, is there danger, is it imminent, what is the cause, for what reasons, why? A small peaceable country. We shall see on Sunday, Sunday will decide—little does the Emperor of China know what will be decided on Sunday, of course he doesn't know a thing.

Li Tai-po and Tu Fu, as realised by the poetry enthusiast Aristide Lapiné. Wild geese flying over distant Mongolia, distant Tibet—another mountainous country. . . .

Meanwhile Monti and Lapiné contemplate the beautiful proportions of the music-room. Still *Jugendstil*, of course, but hardly any ornamentation. One can overlook the ornament here, as Bruno Frischherz once said (adding with a giggle, if one doesn't look too closely), the room is such a perfectly proportioned cube. After which he made a speech in praise of the architect of the Tedesco villa, in his opinion the greatest architectural genius of the twentieth century. The house is built up of cubes, Frischherz explains, no surface is veiled, each shows up clearly as a single word and a part of the whole, made up out of equal words. This perfectly constructed sentence projects a meaning which has been steadily apparent since the very creation of the building. Herein lies the power of a true work of art, an eternal good example. . . . After this digression in memory of the absent Frischherz—a totally apolitical artist, but more or less associated with left-wing circles—the chamber music could begin, with Schubert's Opus 327, it's about time.

Monti and Lapiné have finished their third glass of the light Vöslauer, but Ricki Tedesco is still waiting for the dramatist Zwillinger to arrive. He is obviously late, but manages to arrive just before the first stroke of the quintet, flushed like a rose, throwing his arms up in the air, kissing hands, Zwillinger is in the highest of spirits. As though drunk, but in fact perfectly sober, he runs into the music-room and sits down beside Ricki.

I'm late because I couldn't get through the crowded streets quickly enough, enthusiastic crowds everywhere, nobody shouting 'Heil Hitler!' The decisive question has been posed : Do you want to live without Hitler? Answer : Yes !

Bravo, says Monti to Lapiné, that marks the turning-point, the guarantees from the big brothers, France, England, Italy too, are all ready. We no longer stand alone, bravo ! He claps his hands and calls through the room : Hitler stay in your Reich !

Good news from the provinces, too, Zwillinger continues. The Tyrolese are as merry as ever and looking forward to Sunday—the same goes for Vorarlberg, only Graz is still playing up. But the Reds are very strong there, and they've made it up with us—whereupon Schubert's Opus 327 begins.

Vienna will always be Vienna, Ricki just has time to whisper, then the piano-trout begin their somersaulting about the room, darting to and fro, twisting about like musical diagrams past the ears of Monti, Lapiné and Zwillinger, hiding behind the strings, emerging again, as though they had lain concealed behind round, sun-dappled pebbles in the green waters of the Traun, leaping up and diving down. Monti closes his eyes, thinking of summer, the Traun River, the Salzkammergut, where the trout do indeed dart about in green shallow streams. Even if the Nazis take over Vienna, Monti thinks, they will be Viennese Nazis, they won't become sharp-edged Prussians. In spite of everything, Vienna always will be Vienna. What does for Berlin wouldn't go down here.

Monti wakes from his reverie during the second's complete silence between the last violin note and the first sound of clapping. Get up, attend to Lapiné, make Zwillinger tell it all over again : Excited crowds everywhere, but not a soul crying 'Heil Hitler'. Then out on to the terrace with Ricki, look down upon the Danube metropolis, the watershed, *urbs ventosa,* sybarite town, Jewish town, Czech town, German town (and according to Metternich's *bon mot,* Asia begins on the highway of the Third District)—look down on the brightly lit city. Illuminated partly by electric street lamps, and partly still by the old gas lamps. *A gas lamp is an object that lights the street, but in a man's political life it can be one of the Last Things, if for instance he is suspended from one.* One can be hanged just as well from an electric street lamp as from an old-fashioned gas lamp. Ridiculous thoughts about the possibilities of street lamps ancient and modern, especially ridiculous on a pre-spring night like this, with this luminous crescent of Danube at one's feet, the water surface reflecting starlight as well as street lamplight. Above it all the spire of St Stephen's with the watchman's light burning. There is always a fire-man up there to report any fire that breaks out in this sybarite town, Jewish town, Czech town, German town—so one learns at school.

Monti, Zwillinger and Lapiné are enchanted, and they toast each other on this terrace with the marvellous view before returning to the music-room. Here Ricki Tedesco has meanwhile had a lectern set up, complete with standard lamp, water-jug and tumbler.

Ladies and gentlemen, she announces, Monsieur Aristide Lapiné, that good friend of Austria, will now give us some samples of his translations of Goethe's poems into French.

Aristide Lapiné concludes his reading at the Tedesco villa, not unreasonably, with his masterpiece as a translator, the 'Watchman's Song' from *Faust, Part Two*:

Né pour regarder
Préposé pour contempler

Consacré à la tour
Le monde me plaît.

Je regarde dans le lointain
Je vois de près
La lune et les étoiles
La forêt et les chevreuils
Ainsi je vois partout, l'éternelle beauté des choses
Et comme elle me plaît, je me plais ainsi moi-même.

Yeux! Yeux bienheureux!
Qui avez vu cela quoique cela aît pu être
C'était pourtant si beau.

Ricki Tedesco is justifiably well pleased with this lovely ending to her lovely evening. As are Monti, Lapiné and Zwillinger. The Tedesco salon remains the most distinguished in town, as regards entertainment, as regards the standing of the guests—and in every way.

The wealth of pleasures offered was once again quite unique, Ricki, unbeatable, says Monti in farewell, *Ich küss' die Hände.*

Tomorrow he will send her azaleas.

8 Five short Interludes (I-V) which are actually five short afterpieces

I. *Enter Uncle Rudi*

Who hasn't put in an appearance so far. No wonder : as a member of an underground organisation, the Neighbour's brother-in-law and unemployed, he enters pretty softly, doesn't want to draw attention to himself, treads pretty warily, one false step could blow his organisation, the Comrades, sky-high.

The days of official excursions to the Wienerwald, week-end outings with 20,000 comrades, 20,000 Reds in full hiking gear, but with peaked cap, chinstrap, machine-gun parts in the family rucksack—those days are long past, the caps have been taken off, thrown away or shot away, sometimes the head got shot away at the same time, a William Tell shot with slight extra curvature of the ballistic hyperbola.

Machine-gun parts are still around, but no longer in the family rucksack. They are kept in more secret places: under coke heaps in coal cellars, in rabbit hutches on box balconies, under compost heaps on allotments. They are kept well oiled, however. Uncle Rudi has hidden his gun under a stack of old parquet floorboards in the cellar. He relays parquet flooring as an occasional worker—that is, when there is occasion to work. Usually there isn't. But there is always a pile of old parquet floorboards about, sometimes new ones as well, nobody suspects the gun underneath.

Who, for that matter, suspects anything extraordinary under Uncle Rudi's check shirt? Other than a consumptive chest, that is. Every other Viennese journeyman-carpenter has had the choice of T.B. or cirrhosis—some chose both. Uncle Rudi is a carpenter by profession, Uncle Rudi is the eighth child of impoverished parents, I might well visualise a consumptive chest under that check shirt without collar or tie, I might well suppose a drunkard's liver under his grey trousers (the knees are frayed from sliding about laying floorboards).

But when I ask about something extraordinary, I mean a thick envelope containing a thick bundle of green hundred-dollar notes. He wears it on a string around his neck, for his first-ever journey to the Riviera—to Spain, actually. An unemployed Viennese worker, or occasional worker, from the Pfefferhofgasse, on his first trip to the Mediterranean, sees the painters' country between Avignon and Arles, says That's beautiful, and warm too, even in February (without a *putsch*) or in March (March without detention camp), and he has a thick envelope with greenbacks suspended round his neck. It would of course be something out of the ordinary if he were to change these dollars for chips at the Casino in Nice or Monte Carlo and try his luck—a really thrilling adventure story that would be.

But nothing so exciting happens. Uncle Rudi doesn't get off, doesn't appear in Nice or Monte Carlo, continues third class to Toulon and Biarritz, and when crossing the border to Spain lets the sealed envelope dangle free on a string above the rails (the string being fastened to the lid of the carriage lavatory), gets the money safely across the border, still doesn't spend it beyond the Pyrenees, either on chips or on bullfights, but in a coffee-house in Zaragoza he hands it to a Spanish comrade, saying, Here's a bit of powder and shot to fire up the Caudillo's arse, with best wishes from your Viennese comrades. Friendship!

After his return from the Spanish and French Riviera, having seen the artists' country between Avignon and Arles, does this mysterious Rudi go to his pile of parquet floor-boards in the cellar, take out his gun, polish it, oil it, contact that trusty friend for the first time since February 1934,* with the intention of shooting clay pigeons in the Wienerwald? Or intending at long last to put a bullet through the cardinal's hat of the Lord Cardinal Archbishop of Vienna during the procession? Or does he just want to take a pot-shot at the beautiful glass-clear March sky over Vienna?

At dawn on Friday, 11th March, 1938, on the Schmelz terrain, does he join his comrades of the underground detachment just to shake hands with them? Let me call this early morning expedition, Uncle Rudi's rallying to the last Imperial Manœuvres of the First Republic, for suddenly all three nations of the country—the Red, the Black and the Black and Yellow**—are all there, standing to attention. Just look at that. The wind which blows perpetually over the Schmelz has gathered up the followers of Old Prohaska (Prohaska I and Franz Joseph I, the Siamese twins), and the lads wearing felt hats with cock's tail-feathers, and Uncle Rudi's comrades, and blown them all with one great gust via Oeverseegasse, Gablenzgasse and

* Time of the Austrian Civil War between Socialists and militant Catholic right-wingers, ending in the suppression of the Socialist Party.

** Red = Socialists; black = Catholic right wing; black and yellow = Monarchists.

Johnstrasse, to this meeting-point—sound the assembly, then, with the 'Radetzky March' perhaps. *(My pretty child, I love you true, My feathered hat salutes you too.)*

Or with the Internationale, *Then comrades, come rally, and the last fight let us face!*

Or what else? The *Neue Freie Presse** of 1897 describes the spring manœuvres on the Schmelz territory thus: 'A glorious spring morning, the like of which we have not yet seen this season, began the day. Not a cloud in the sky, not a breeze over the plain, and the sun put forth his gentle rays, flooding with light the splendid spectacle that unfolded on the Schmelz parade ground.'

Why hark back to all that? But what could I have done? Could I help Uncle Rudi, could I support the Prohaska Loyalists, could I be of any use to the cock's feather brigade, could I change my Nursery Self into a General Staff Self? They're all waiting here for marching and shooting orders, On your marks, get set, go! against Adolf Hitler—but a four-year-old can give neither marching nor shooting orders, least of all against Adolf Hitler.

On that last Friday the First Republic still has a whole day to go, although in fact a republic has been forbidden for the last four years, and Uncle Rudi makes his entrance in order to exchange the dummy bullets for live ones in these last Imperial Manœuvres of the First Republic—but the bullets never get fired.

The very next morning there was Adolf Hitler pressing a gigantic bunch of flowers (a Little Red Riding Hood with pigtails handed it to him at the border) to his toothbrush moustache.

* Most influential paper under the Monarchy, liberal yet loyal to the established order.

II. *Frau Josephine Wimmer wants to mount Prince Eugene's Bronze Horse but only reaches the lower parts*

Josephine Wimmer does not get into the Old Town all that often, though her husband does have a bookshop there. The husband in his business premises, the wife in the garden suburb villa, the wife at the stove, the wife looking after her child, fourteen-year-old Wilhelm Theodor Wimmer, to be precise—good order begins in the home.

It used to come from above—God the Father, archangels, angels, God's Secretary of State, clothed in white, in Rome, the latter's Cardinal Archbishop in Vienna—or else Wotan, heathen Saxon kings, Turnvater Jahn*—order, right down to the bank manager. Who should, damn it all, look after the Wimmer family's savings properly, keep loan stock bonds in order so that they don't go down in value. Frau Josephine Wimmer is thinking particularly of the fourth tax-free issue 5½ per cent Austrian War Loan of 1916 in 1,000-kronen batches, a bundle of which she brought by way of dowry. Now Willi Theodor cuts toy soldiers out of the thick, worthless paper.

Order must come from below, then, from the smallest cells of the State, the New Order will have to start from below, until there is a Top again, until one is up again—like the twenty-man pyramid in front of the Chancelry.

Twenty athletic Illegal Party members have been practising this twenty-man pyramid in the Wienerwald; now it stands with its back to the Heldenplatz (the Heroes' Square), at last emerged from the shadows of the Wienerwald into the splendid bright March sun. Heads forward,

* Nineteenth-century Teutonic hero, who equated physical exercise with patriotic virtue.

torsos braced, shoulders serving as platforms, the strongest Illegal ones at the bottom, one man climbing on another's shoulders, the human pyramid grows, towards the bulging balcony of the baroque palace, reaching out and stretching, forming a base for the tip, which materialises in the shape of a feather- or flyweight, this feather- (or fly)weight scrambles up the back of the human pyramid, the very smallest and lightest Illegal member they could find—the flag with the antique German cross-spider rolled up like a haversack on his back—the swastika standard-bearer scrambles up until he can form the tip of the pyramid, a little uncertain, a slight reed in the March wind, he stands upright at the top, but not quite at the top yet, for now, hup, he leaps on to the balcony. It is the greatest March day of party member Tom Thumb's little life, he leaps from the balcony's stone parapet down to the balcony itself, turns round—Bravo, *Heil, Sieg Heil!* the Pyramid shouts—and now party member Featherlight unrolls his blood-red flag luggage.

Why do these unnatural events always take place on balconies? New forms of State are always proclaimed from balconies, on principle—which is why nowadays I only rent apartments without balconies.

In any case, Bruno Wimmer watched the erection of this Viennese Cheops Pyramid minutely. By rights he should not be strolling about the Old Town on a Saturday, on such a sunny March day he should really be sitting, for the first time this year perhaps, in the garden of the Pötzleinsdorf multifamily villa with Frau Josephine Wimmer, albeit without having done the fair day's work that deserves the fair day's pay—no Cross, no Crown—the silver tray with the snow-white tray-cloth in front of him, initials J.W., Josephine Wimmer, and on it coffee, a sugary bun and a glass of water. But it was still too cold for a leisurely snack in the garden. In any case Bruno Wimmer has no intention of sitting in the garden on this particular Saturday, or in the apartment with Josephine and Willi Theodor, for that matter.

Instead he stands enraptured with his back to the Heldenplatz, watching the pyramid, how it grows, how it reaches upwards, how athletically it is scaled and finally crowned. *Heil Hitler, Sieg Heil!* Now at last Wimmer dares to take out the beloved party badge, too long concealed by Josephine at home beneath snow-white tray-cloths marked J.W. in the linen chest, from his upper coat pocket. He pins it to his lapel and swells his chest.

At this moment faith in the future returns so marvellously to Wimmer, courses so powerfully through his blood, that Josephine sees in his eyes, not just from his jacket lapel, what has happened, when he comes home. She embraces him passionately as on their wedding night and, together with Bruno Wimmer, so to speak, Adolf Hitler, desired not only by a hundred thousand men in Vienna but by a hundred thousand Viennese women as well, presses him to her, the part symbol of the whole, *Heil Bruno Wimmer!*

During these March days Josephine Wimmer ceases for once to be a careful housekeeper, to keep accounts. She feels a delicious intoxication without benefit of wine, or even youth : by the Heldenplatz in Vienna the lilac blooms again every year for lovers. She will mount the bronze horse of Prinz Eugene, Prince Eugene that noble knight, Had a bridge built up by night, Had his men go up and down, O'er the bridge and through the town.*

* Folk-song celebrating Prince Eugene's decisive victory over the Turks at Belgrade.

What is the German Fatherland, is't Prussia—Swabia, Bavaria, or Styria? Oh true, 'tis also Austria, glorious and victorious, wants to mount the bronze horse, certainly not to look down on industrialists, famous advocates, successful artists, foreigners, gamblers and Jews—of whom there may not even be any in this crowd of thousands upon thousands of cheering masses between the statues of Prince Eugene and Archduke Karl.

No, from that horse she wants to look into the eyes of Adolf Hitler, the man desired, as aforesaid, by a hundred thousand Viennese women, as he stands on the balcony of the new Hofburg—yet another balcony, My kingdom for a town without balconies, where they could never proclaim new states from balconies!—raises his hand in greeting to Josephine Wimmer, come into her own after the villa's suburban loneliness, with one piercing look into her eyes resolves her loneliness, ends it, brings her final satisfaction. To look into his eyes: that is why she wants to mount Prince Eugene's horse of bronze. But she only gets as far as the tail end, like so many others, climbing the pedestal of the monument, letting themselves be drawn up, mostly young lads, adolescents, athletes in white singlets, they help Josephine Wimmer up too, draw her up, make room for her on the first step of the pedestal. But she climbs on, a March day without thought for the family, reaches the bronze base plate of the equestrian statue, but no farther.

The bronze Prince's horse, as I have mentioned, waves its forelegs about in the air, if Josephine Wimmer had got any farther she would certainly have fallen off the horse's sloping back—anyhow, it's facing the wrong way for Adolf Hitler's speaker's balcony, the victor of Belgrade is turning his back on Him, so Josephine would have had to turn round as well to look into the Führer's eyes—nevertheless she keeps trying, on this blue March day, to mount Prince Eugene's horse completely, and again and again she can only get as far as the tail end.

Meanwhile the Führer has begun his speech, and now with his hypnotic gaze he holds Josephine Wimmer spell-bound under the bronze tail, so that she forgets all about climbing on.

III. *Bruno Wimmer drags Sailor Boy into the 'Mutzenbacher Cabinet', thus rendering him last aid*

Of course one should not utter the name 'Mutzenbacher' these days or in these circumstances—those confessions of a houri, famous on Graben Kärtnerstrasse, Ring-Rund and Kohlmarkt, splendidly natural if somewhat lascivious reading for humanists in these unnatural times.*

If only the police were as prepared to turn a blind eye on secret voluptuaries—who are, moreover, willing to pay for their vices—as they did on Adolf Hitler's spies, free-thinkers or the apparently pious, yesterday still fawning on the Cardinal Archbishop, yet at the same time already planning to sack his residence; on respectable Jew-baiters, members of the Austrian Legion just returned home, their sharpshooters' eyes cheerfully surveying the serried windows of those beautiful apartments as yet still inhabited by opponents of Adolf Hitler (true, they are hiding now with curtains drawn), but already marked out for these same

* A reference to the pornographic novel, *Josefine Mutzenbacher*, a Viennese Fanny Hill, legally unobtainable, and almost certainly written by Felix Salten, author of *Bambi*.

winking sharpshooters; on ministers whose high treason will be rewarded with bouquets and even with the Chancellor's seat,* a mere two-months' Chancellor seat, to be sure. Suppose, during these uncertain March days (Danger has crossed the border, but just how great is this danger, against whom will it be directed first, who will be allowed to stay, who will be exiled, who will lose his life and who will only lose his shirt? And the big brothers, those humanists of the League of Nations—Peace on earth to men of good will, or any sort of will—will they follow up their spirited telegrams—*His Majesty's Government cannot take responsibility for advising the Chancellor to take any course of action which might expose his country to dangers against which His Majesty's Government is unable to guarantee protection*—with equally spirited letters of protest?), suppose the police were even willing to close both eyes, as that chronically handicapped figure of Justice on the left-hand gable of Parliament has always done? Would Bruno Wimmer still have to rush out like a lunatic from his bookshop and seize Sailor Boy (who after all hasn't been Wimmer's partner for ages now) as he walks past in the direction of the Graben, grab him by his lapels and drag him into the bookshop, open a door at the back into the packing department, open a second door, which leads into the so-called 'Mutzenbacher Cabinet', hurriedly slam the door upon this cabinet, turn the key in the lock from the outside and run away?

Meanwhile the frightened Sailor Boy stands in the 'Mutzenbacher Cabinet', and the first thing he does is switch the light on. This back room of the bookshop has no windows, it is a secret room, a room where the shelves do not harbour *The Collected Poems of Eichendorff*, or

* Refers to Seyss-Inquart.

Stifter's *Nachsommer*, not even *All Quiet on the Western Front* or *Berlin Alexanderplatz*, but various footnotes and postscripts to the natural, if somewhat lewd, world of lust. Beautifully bound and numbered private copies, Lucian's *Dialogues with Hetaerae*, illustrated *Histories of Morals*, *The Female Nude in Art*, *A Cultural History of Temple Prostitution*, *The Confessions of a Parisian Fille de Joie as Told by a Former Jesuit Father*—and of course the Mutzenbacherin.

Only personally recommended, discreet old customers are admitted here. The biggest customer attraction of the Cabinet, a sort of hand-operated peepshow as in better-class Prater establishments, but not showing photographic sequences like *The Seventy-Seven Wonders of the Old and the New World*, 80 groschen, or *A Journey from the North to the South Pole, 25 pictures from the Genuine Expedition*, 60 groschen—no, far from it: ladies, nothing but ladies. And who knows how little they're wearing, and who knows whether they are in fact ladies. Be that as it may, many an elderly industrialist has had Wimmer's Peepshow Wheel of Beauty—acquired while Sailor Boy was still a partner—revealed to him, murmuring to himself, hasn't she got a gorgeous ——, and felt exceedingly wicked.

Why has Bruno Wimmer locked Sailor Boy in this windowless room? He could, of course, forget the unnatural outside world here, or at least try to forget it. But unfortunately he knows all this stock already, and why the devil doesn't Wimmer come back even after half an hour, unlock the door and explain his crazy behaviour? Why does Wimmer only come back an hour later, pale, somewhat agitated, take Sailor Boy by the shoulders and say shakily, Don't you understand, they're combing the streets and catching Jews to sweep the streets with their bare hands. Now they've gone, you can go on again.

What'll we do with the Jews?
We've got news
For those rich Jews
They'll have to sweep the streets!

Twenty years ago—Long live the Republic!—they sang a similar song, to the same old tune:

What'll we do with the nobles?
The noble class
With all their brass
They'll have to sweep the streets!

But if all the rich are going to sweep the streets, who will remain to soil them? The doves of peace from the Rathaus Park, the telltale-tits from the Volksgarten, perhaps—do allegorical birds have a normal digestion? What they ought to do is arrange quickly for the Municipal Import of Refuse, but that has nothing to do with Sailor Boy or with Bruno Wimmer either.

IV. *Gusti Wawra's father becomes somebody, as I can see on the Pötzleinsdorfer Strasse*

A four-year-old doesn't get around much. He would need to make the equivalent of a Grand Tour, to see Great Uncle Rudi, gun taken out from under the pile of parquet floorboards, standing to attention, at dawn on the Schmelz, waiting in vain for the order to march or shoot. Or Frau Josephine Wimmer on the Heldenplatz, wanting to mount Prince Eugene's bronze horse, but only getting as far as the lower parts. Or watch Sailor Boy being dragged off into the 'Mutzenbacher Cabinet' for his own good, by way of rendering him last aid.

A Grand Tour of one's own birthplace, led at one's nanny's hand perhaps, to admire the last contingent, no longer Red but ash-grey, of an underground resistance that failed to prove a phoenix, on the former Imperial parade ground; to a musical accompaniment of songs that were never children's songs: 'Then on the Schmelz the fun will start. . . .' Or to sight the houseowner's wife Josephine Wimmer almost as high up, though facing the wrong way, as Prince Eugene himself. And then see Sailor Boy vanish from the street at lightning speed, as in a trick film.

'That,' says the paediatrician, 'would be the surest way to make this boy, who is already rather pale, a complete nervous wreck. Continue as before to give him two table-spoons of carrot juice three times a day before meals.'

What the hell do you mean, continue as before? After Uncle Rudi's bottomless disappointment that, even in bright daylight, no orders came, cannot be as before Josephine Wimmer's final complete loss of voice, as after hours of cheering the attention of former lance-corporal Adolf Hitler (badly burned by a lewisite combination in 1918) is still not turned to her alone but to all the many thousands cheering between Prince Eugene's horse and Archduke Karl's horse. Before Bruno Wimmer's unspeak-able joy at the sight of the unfurled flag with the antic German cross-spider, or after his rendering last aid?

All that, before and after, later or earlier, before the

seizure of power and afterwards, behind and before, hither and yon, I had to piece together laboriously for myself, much later. Everybody is always demanding that the young should take an interest in contemporary events, yet they are always kept away from them. 'After' should mean, after the complete reannexation of my black-eyed children's, or rather childhood, home town to the blonde mother country between Upper Danube and Lower Rhine—the historic German rebellion against Rome under Hermann in the Teutoburg Forest now marks the new Year Nought —that wonderful mother country between the Zugspitze and Kilimanjaro (later I learnt to read, merely to learn from the Annual Calendar of the German Colonial Federation that the highest mountain in Greater Germany is Kilimanjaro). . . .

Does my dawning consciousness detect something wrong with me, although I am still getting my two tablespoons of carrot juice three times a day as before? As we are going out for our morning walk, why does my nanny stop longer than usual talking to the housekeeper Frau Jellinek? The two women whisper, point up towards Sailor Boy's apartment, look at me in a funny way, understandable impatience on my part, as I stand there with my toy spade, toy bucket, toy rake and sand moulds, a miniature *homo ludens* who doesn't understand the situation and begins to whine, a spoilt brat, thinking only of worms which he wants to dig out of the Schafberg clay, together with Gusti Wawra.

Gusti waits every day by the wrought-iron gate of the Schönbrunn-yellow painted villa in the Pötzleinsdorfer Strasse, for me to come with my nanny. Today his father is waiting with him, he has put a funny button on the lapel of his coat, a button with a red rim and two pin-men sitting on a seesaw. Whichever way you turn the button, one little pin-man has his head up and the other has his head down, a funny sort of seesaw. One little man might bang his head on the ground. But there is no buttonhole. This sort of button is in fact the Swastika badge, which confirms officially that Herr Wawra is made of the right (full carat) party alloy.

My nanny stops politely in front of Gusti Wawra's father, although he shoots his arm up as though to catch her nose. Only he doesn't clench his fist like a fly- or nose-catcher, but keeps his arm standing in the air as if in a splint, clicks his heels together and calls *'Heil Hitler'*, a pretty unskilled nose- *or* fly-catcher.

Then Gusti's father speaks softly to my nanny and takes Gusti's hand; but Nanny is to take Gusti and me to the Schafberg, on her hand. But he will not let go of Gusti's hand, and it is without Gusti that my nanny takes me along the Pötzleinsdorfer Strasse and to the Schafberg. I've got to dig for earthworms all by myself: but those two old people needn't have made such a fuss about that.

V. *An apartment becomes Lebensraum*

that is, 'room to expand'—which the legionary Richard Widenzky claims as his right, and among other things he means my nursery. He also means the living-room, and the bedroom of Sailor Boy and his wife, the lovely sunny corner-room rented to Gogo Gutmann as well as my nanny's *kabinett*, the hall, the kitchen, the bathroom. And very sensibly he also claims the lavatory as 'room to expand'.

To the fully grown legionary,* my nursery is no more than the political beer-cellar was to the Warden of the New Order between the upper reaches of the Danube (meanwhile become the Middle Danube) and lower reaches of the Rhine, that New Order between the Zugspitze (now yielding place to Grossglockner) and Kilimanjaro: a mere political beginning; but then, the beginning is always the most difficult part, and at least Widenzky has got that over.

To leave wife and child, move over into the blonde mother country, be called up, put in line, trained, in the Austrian Legion. Polish boots, clean your gun and point it eastwards, blanco your belt, polish the buttons on your uniform, practise assault, set your sights across horizon and corn to the border, look enviously at the natural corn beyond the border, flourishing under the tinkling of consecrated church bells, apparently also under Talmudic blessing, on the cultivated fields of the One-Party Republic. Sing *'Die Fahne hoch, die Reihen fest geschlossen . . .'*** and in the evening read the Bible of the New Order. Why did the imprisonment in Landsberg have to be so long? Widenzky would have preferred the book to be shorter, indeed a few easily memorised headings would have sufficed him.

The Aryans, True Founders of Culture; Do Not Overburden Young Brains; Fear of Chauvinism the Sign of Impotence; Leadership and the Masses; Anti-Prussianism a Diversionary Manœuvre; Area in Relation to World Power; No More Sentimentality in Diplomatic Relations;

* Member of the Austrian Legion being trained in Germany for the take-over of Austria.

** Horst Wessel song (Nazi anthem): 'Raise up the flag, and keep our ranks together.'

Using Our Philosophy to Attack; Concentrating on the Real Enemy.

That would be quite enough to write on a bomb delivered to the archepiscopal palace with the morning's bakeries, laid on the rails of express lines, laid like wreaths of cornflowers round the pylons of high-tension cables, sluiced with the melted snows into the high-pressure water mains, into the high-power generators—speed the plough, speed the plough, the tomtit calls in spring, according to peasant tradition. Then it's high time, not only to get out plough and harrow, but to search the munitions bags for gorgeous white dynamite and scatter it over the landscape. In Widenzky's eyes these spring bombs are the true available incense vessels for the true full-blooded Sunday masses, which can literally make an angel of the most stubborn opponent. Widenzky's censers are no longer needed at present.

To return to one's native country, showered with flowers under a glass-clear March sky, with Adolf Hitler's panzers, with the Governor's guns, covered by the fighter planes of the Leader, with a calm firm tread—that marks a really convincing victory over the inferior races, one doesn't have to have been a legionary in order to become, finally and unconditionally, that Leader's follower.

Now then, says Widenzky at the telephone outside my nursery—it is fixed to the wall and Gusti Wawra and I have often tried to reach it, but it hangs too high for children—now then, can I at last have a word with District Group Leader Wawra, *Heil Hitler*, mission accomplished, apartment searched, condition perfect, windows freshly painted, new parquet floors, overlooks the garden. Thanks—I'll hang on to it.